# THE ARCOLOGY

Carlyle Edmundson

To my family and my writing club,
each indispensable in their own way.

## Table of Contents

## <u>Void of the Net</u>

Soft shadows fell across the room as the neon signs outside flickered to life. The muted beats from the techno club across the street wafted through the venetian blinds of my corner office. I hadn't had a case worth taking in weeks, and today was no different. I reached into the bottom drawer of my desk and retrieved a small glass and a half-full bottle of Scotch. I was all ready to grab my book, kick my feet up on the desk and call it a day when a stunning silhouette appeared in the frosted glass.

The door creaked open, revealing the alluring figure responsible: a woman in a black dress so tight I could practically read the label. The way she carried herself gave it a sense of class and dignity that few others would be able to pull off. Crimson curls lined her face, obscured by thick sunglasses completely out of place on a dreary November day like this. Everything I'd ever read told me a woman like this was trouble, through and through. As she removed her mirrored shades, I caught sight of deep green eyes darting back and forth, like gemstones set against reddened and glistening cheeks.

"Excuse me, but... you're a detective, right?" she asked. Her voice was restrained, held back by uncertainty with a dash of fear, and in an instant my impression was shattered. This girl wasn't the femme fatale I was hoping for.

"Lance Canela, at your service," I replied, gesturing to the vacant seat across the desk. She sat down on the faded couch in the corner near the door. The slow moving ceiling fan made its presence known as she smoothed out the wrinkles in her dress.

"Quite a... retro... office you have here." She looked around the darkened room, taking in the old bookshelves and furniture. "Would it be alright if I turned up the lights?"

"If you must." I sat upright and pulled my chair into the desk as the lights kicked on. So much for my carefully cultivated atmosphere. "What can I do for you, Miss...?"

"Fiona MacLeod. I came down here to check on my brother, but I..." her voice trailed off. She took a deep breath and retrieved a photo from a tiny purse. After staring at it for a moment, she walked over and slid it across the desk. It was a picture of a young man, barely an adult, with her same red hair. "That's Logan, though he's a bit older than that now. I'm sorry I couldn't find a more recent picture; he couldn't stand having them taken."

I picked up the Scotch and offered her a glass, but she waved it away. I poured one for myself and put it back in the drawer.

"I got a letter from him in the mail about three weeks ago," Fiona continued, "but nothing since. He didn't seem particularly concerned."

"Mail, huh? Pretty unusual these days." I leaned back and looked out the window. The club-goers were just starting to line up outside in their outlandish costumes, grotesque shadows outlined by the glowing wire embedded in their clothes. Long winter nights just meant more time to party for them.

"He... didn't really trust electronic communication." She shifted uncomfortably, passing the purse from her left hand to the right. "I was planning to see him today, and hopefully talk him into coming home for the holidays. But when I got down to his apartment, he didn't answer. I wasn't able to get the door open, either."

"I'm gonna need a little more than that. What's he do for a living? Hobbies? Any enemies, or people that might want him out of the way?"

"Logan was a computer consultant," Fiona said. She glanced down at the picture with a sigh. "Or at least, that's what he'd tell our mother. I'm not so sure that his 'consulting' was always wanted, however."

"So he's a hacker." No point in dancing around the facts. "Hacking's a high class felony these days. He could've been pinched by the Feds for that."

"You see why I can't go to the police, then." Fiona brushed aside a stray lock of those thick red curls. "Can you take the case?"

"I can, but I have a feeling you're not gonna like what I find. Still interested?" I needed the business, but there was no point in making the girl suffer.

"Yes. If he's hurt, or worse... then I need something to tell our parents. I can't hide the truth from them forever." She shuffled through her purse for a moment before producing a set of keys. "Here. These are the spares to his apartment. The address is on the key chain. Maybe you can find something there; I'm not sure I want to try. I'll give you my contact information as well, so keep me updated on your findings."

"I'll get on it first thing in the morning. We'll discuss payment at a later date," I said as I stood up and took the keys.

"Well then. Good night, Mister Canela." Fiona walked out of my office, her shadow once again gliding along the frosted panes until passing out of view. I donned my fedora and trench coat, locked up, and set off for home. Out of curiosity, I checked the address on the keys. The kid's apartment happened to be just a few blocks from here. I decided it might be worth a quick look and made a detour.

The sky rumbled with approaching thunder, momentarily drowning out the sounds of traffic a few blocks back. I looked up and saw the sign for the kid's building. It was coated in a layer of filth, and half the windows on the lower floors were busted out, clumsily covered with cardboard. The lobby wasn't much better; the wallpaper was peeling in places, revealing the stained surface underneath. For a moment, I wondered how his sister appeared so wealthy, while he lived like this. I decided it wasn't worth taking a chance with the elevator and headed upstairs.

The kid's apartment was on the fifth floor, which was dead silent. As I approached, I heard a crash come from inside the room. No wonder Miss Fiona didn't want to look; the lock was badly damaged, as though it had been broken and then hastily put back together to hide that fact. I put my ear to the door and listened carefully. There were at least two men inside, their mumbling just barely audible through the thin walls. I retreated back to the stairwell and decided to watch from afar.

A few minutes later, the two men emerged, wearing finely tailored suits that no one living here could possibly afford. The taller of the pair stopped and slid a hammer into his jacket, while the other knelt down and tried halfheartedly to fix the door lock once again. The tall one tapped his foot impatiently, then shook his head and yanked his far scrawnier partner to his feet, dragging him off to the elevator. Once I was sure they were gone, I approached the apartment.

I managed to open the busted door and went inside. The place was largely barren, but what little furniture was present had been ransacked, and from the looks of it, more than once. The couch was ripped apart, with stuffing all over the floor, and the food had been emptied from the still-open fridge, which cast an eerie light across the room. I cautiously proceeded into what should have been the bedroom. Instead, I entered a hacker's cave, covered wall-to-wall in high-tech computer equipment. The room was littered with computer parts, although the layer of dust led me to believe that the men weren't responsible for this mess. I opened a few drawers, on the off chance that they had missed some clues. Finding them empty, I turned my attention to the computer atop the desk. I followed the wires down from a massive screen to what appeared to be the main computer. The case was open, revealing the absence of several critical components. I tried to put it back together as best I could and turned the machine on.

"Primary hard drive not found," the computer flashed across the screen. "Attempting to boot from secondary…"

I raised an eyebrow and looked inside the machine. There was no sign of a hard drive, which could only mean one thing: he'd hidden a remote backup somewhere nearby. I tried to follow the other wires out the back—no dice. The computer monitor displayed a signal icon in the lower right, which was strong. The remote couldn't be far.

It's operational, and it can't possibly be running off a battery, given how long the kid's been missing. I searched the apartment for any inconspicuous wall sockets. As my search led me to the kitchen, I noticed the refrigerator's power cord was stretched almost to its limit. I closed the fridge and pulled it away from the wall; behind it was a section of drywall that had clearly been patched, but not yet repainted. I dug through the drawers until I found a knife and carefully cut away the panel. Sure enough, hidden inside the wall was a detached outlet and a thin, flat hard drive, with a small antenna emerging from the end. I removed it from its hiding spot and pocketed it, revealing the paper underneath. It was a handwritten letter, addressed to Fiona. I folded it carefully and tucked it in my coat pocket. After setting the kitchen back how I'd found it, I shut off the computer, locked up as well as I could, and left.

I walked home under the feeble glare of the streetlights. The clouds had moved in, rolling and streaming around the tops of the surrounding skyscrapers. This part of the city lived in their shadows each day, until night returned and darkness could reclaim the rest.

I took off my coat and hat, tossing them onto the couch in the cramped living room. As I prepared a package of instant ramen, I decided to take a look at the letter. The contents were more or less what you'd expect: it discussed his everyday life, and why he had cut ties with their well-off family to live alone (to keep them from getting wrapped up in his illicit life), ending with a message for Fiona to pass on to their parents. A perfectly ordinary letter, except for the numbers scattered throughout the first paragraph, completely irrelevant to the text. I copied them down line by line, hoping to spot a pattern, but to no avail. I set the letter aside for the night.

I sat down on the couch with my bowl of noodles, knees pushed up against a coffee table that really didn't belong in a space this tight. I started up some music—ska, from the fifth wave revival a few years back—and stared at the bookshelf across from me, where most people would keep a television. It had begun to dawn on me exactly how dangerous tonight had actually been; if I'd taken the elevator upstairs, there was no way I'd have been able to hide from those two men. Maybe I'd have been able to talk my way out of it, but that had never been my strong suit. I didn't even have a gun on me, if it came down to defending myself. I was far too reckless today, and it seemed this case was more serious than I had first anticipated. Had I gotten myself in over my head?

I set the empty bowl on the table and walked around to the shelf. It was lined with old paperbacks from Raymond Chandler, Dashiell Hammett, and so many others. Most of them were the better part of a century old, having once been my grandfather's. As a private detective himself back in the eighties, they ranked among his most prized possessions. Sitting with him after school, he'd never hesitate to share one of his sordid tales of murder and adultery, embellished with so much action that even Mike Hammer would be left in awe.

Of course, the reality of the job was far different, but I didn't know that as a kid, and I never did hear it from him. I understood now why Philip Marlowe always had to specify his disdain for divorce cases, and while dull, they were among the least offensive of the requests I'd received over time. The average person's impression of a private eye these days wasn't the hardboiled man of honor, but rather what Marlowe might call a shyster, someone to hire to dig up dirt on their enemies or shake down the neighbors. That wasn't what I was looking for.

And yet today would've been exactly what I was waiting for all along. I'd read every last one of these books a dozen times since, and even Grandpa's notes in the margins, and yet now it felt like I had learned nothing. Grabbing one off the shelf, I couldn't help but wonder what Philip Marlowe would do in this situation. Keep his guard up, no doubt, and do whatever it took to find the truth. Too bad Grandpa wasn't around to ask.

It was raining in full force the next morning, water sweeping down between the monolithic buildings like untamed rapids carving their way through the mountainside. I searched through a few drawers, looking for something to keep the hard drive safe, when I came across Grandpa's old pistol. I'd never had a reason to carry it before, but after last night, I didn't want to be unarmed when I found one. I packed the hard drive away in a waterproof bag, hid my pistol in my pocket, and set off to find one of my contacts.

I emerged from an automated taxi in the sketchy parts of downtown, near an unmarked building bordering a hole-in-the-wall bar. Inside, I hung my hat on the rack by the door and approached the bartender.

"I need to see Sigil," I said in a low voice, rain still sliding off my coat. He grunted without looking up and pointed me to a staircase near the bathrooms. The door at the top of the steps was locked, with a peephole built in. I knocked loudly to get his attention.

"Keep it down. Who's there?" the muffled baritone behind the door replied.

"Open the door, Wyatt. It's Lance."

"Go away, Lance. I don't want to talk to you, and I sure as hell don't want you in here."

"Is that any way to repay me after everything I went through on your behalf last month? You'd be in the Pen right now if it weren't for me," I called back. He huffed begrudgingly and the door swung open, blasting me with cold air.

"I wouldn't even have had them on my case if I'd just ignored you last time..." he said, standing back. Wyatt was a big man, his waistline spreading out like the borders of the city, and every bit as grimy. His face was partially obscured by his hacker-standard augmented reality goggles, which in turn were covered by his uncouth brown hair.

"Now, now, you know as well as I do that you can't resist checking out the goodies I find." I stepped inside and he locked the door hastily. "Speaking of which, I have something here which I need you to take a look at."

I produced the bag and held up the drive for him to see. Wyatt's nose bunched up.

"A wireless hard drive. Nothing too special about that," he replied.

"Aw, is it too much for the great Sigil to handle? What if I told you this came from another hacker's place?"

Wyatt snatched the bag away and began setting it up.

"Who was it?" he asked from beneath his computer desk. The enormous rig was even more intricate than the one in Logan's apartment. "Maybe Acolyte? I know she lives around here. Could be one of those other Myriad punks, I guess. Or Void? I bet it was Void. Haven't heard from him in nearly a month. Said he was onto something big, though I never bought into it."

"I'm afraid I don't know his screen name, but that is about when he disappeared," I answered. Wyatt emerged from under the desk, his long, disheveled hair covering his face. "What'd you hear?"

"He bragged a lot, but never put up any proof. Swore that he'd gotten into some megacorp's server and found something juicy. I just assumed someone called him out and he slunk away defeated." He brushed the hair out his eyes and sat down. "There. I'm going to try booting from it."

I watched as the screens lit up with the same images I had seen the night before. Wyatt stared on with anticipation, his opinion on "Void" clearly having changed, until his expression soured.

"That's a bit more extreme than I expected. Pinfish cipher on the secondary partition."

"I'm a P.I., not a hacker. Explain it in English."

"Hmmph. It's a very strong encryption. I can break it, but it's going to take time. As in, months."

"I don't have that kind of time. What can you do to speed this up?"

"Well, if this really does belong to Void, there might be one way. He was still something of a novice, so I'm betting he used a key converter to turn some kind of meaningful word or phrase into his encryption key. If you can find that phrase, we can get access to the partition. Otherwise, check back in March."

I thought back on his apartment for a moment. There hadn't been much of anything meaningful there at all. That was when I remembered the strange numbers. "Could this be it?"

"Let me see…" Wyatt took the paper as soon as I had removed it from my pocket and punched the numbers in. "Nope. It's not working."

"That's too bad. I'll see what else I can find," I said, taking it back and heading for the door. "Thanks for the help, Wyatt."

"Yeah, yeah. And don't call me that!" he shouted back. I grabbed my hat and headed out into the downpour outside.

So the kid had been breaking into megacorp databases. Certainly a noble cause, but a dangerous one. Those two goons were probably from some corporation's private security division. Had this company, whichever one it was, been responsible for his disappearance? And if that's true, why wait so long to check his apartment? What could he have found that called for all this anyway? This was turning out far more interesting than it had appeared.

I decided to call Miss Fiona and catch her up. If anyone would be able to guess Logan's password, it was her, and at the very least I could deliver his letter. I called the number she had given me yesterday.

"Hello?"

"Hello. This is Lance, the detective you hired yesterday. I've found something that you should see, and I was hoping I could get you to look at it today."

"Oh… well, you see, I live at the top of the Arcology, so that might be a bit difficult. Let me see how soon I can get down," she said. If she was living there, her family must be even more well off than I thought.

"It's a letter from your brother." There was a pause after that. The heavy kind.

"I see. I'll meet you in thirty minutes at Split Bean Cafe, across from the aerocar port downtown." She hung up quickly.

The cafe was fairly close, just a few blocks over near the business district. It was the kind of place that I'd normally never be able to afford, but it offered a serene, reasonably private atmosphere that drew in the corporate crowd. Fiona arrived shortly after I did, emerging from the taxi with a navy blue umbrella.

"Good morning, Mister Canela," she said as she approached the awning I was standing under. She was wearing another beautiful, expensive dress, but this one was dark and formal, the kind of clothes you'd wear to a funeral—and I'd been to enough of them to know.

"Ah, good morning." I stepped past towards the door, and I could feel her give me the once over.

"I suppose that's one way to deal with the rain." I turned back, and she gestured towards my trench coat.

"Oh, yeah. Hydrophobic coating," I replied, raising an arm. Water droplets struck the coat's sleeve and slid right off without so much as a damp spot. "Shall we head inside?"

I shook off what little water remained, and we sat down at a booth in a quiet corner of the shop. The steady stream of taxis dropping people off and picking them up were just visible through the window.

"So, you've found something from Logan?"

I explained what went down last night, then reached into my coat's inner pocket and retrieved the letter. She plucked it from my hands, and a relieved smile came across her face as she eagerly read through it. Her joy made for a truly wonderful sight, and I could tell what she was thinking: perhaps Logan had skipped town, and left this note for her. Maybe he was just in hiding, and would reemerge in a few weeks when whatever trouble he was in had blown over. In that moment, I desperately hoped it was true, if only for her sake. As she reached the end, she looked up, a puzzled expression on her face.

"Why are there all these numbers? Do they mean something?"

"I was hoping you could tell me. I thought they might be the password for his hard drive, but that wasn't the case." I took the letter and flipped it over. "I wrote them out line by line on the back. Do you recognize any of them?"

Fiona pondered for a moment. My hope for a quick solution was fading fast until she finally spoke up.

"Hmm..." She stared at the numbers intensely. "Well, four-thirty-seven White Oak Lane was the address of the house we grew up in, out in western New York state."

"Keep going."

"I think fifty-one was his uniform number on the soccer team when we were kids, and down here, these last few numbers are the date when he moved into the Arcology." She looked up from the page, eyes wide. "These numbers... I recognize every last one!"

She scribbled down what each one meant onto a napkin. It was a clever ploy; only someone close to Logan could have identified these, and it ensured that someone he trusted could still access the data if it came down to it.

"I remember now, a few years ago. He helped me with my phone security, and one of the things he showed me was how these phrases work. A string of words that only have meaning for you," Fiona said, looking up. Her vibrant green eyes, like discs of etched jade, were begging for hope. "Is this going to help you find him?"

"Yeah, this is real helpful. Thanks," I said as I stood up. I knew there was little chance of finding the poor kid alive, but I couldn't bear to break that reality to her now.

I bid Fiona farewell and set off into the downpour to return to Wyatt's den. It didn't take any coercion this time; he eagerly rushed to the door after hearing what I'd found. Wyatt snatched away the napkin and ran back to his computer, nearly tripping on loose cables.

"Alright, I'll just put them into the cryptography program like so..." he muttered, so low I could just make it out over the computer's cooling system. His face suddenly contorted in disgust. "It's not working. Your info is bogus."

"Do you always give up so quickly?" I asked, yanking the note back. "Look here. Just input the words, not the numbers."

Wyatt complied, and the decryption program emitted a pleasant ding. He snorted again.

"I was getting to that," he said. He flipped through the data, moving from file to file so fast I could hardly keep up. An image came up, displaying a word in stylized font. "Yeah, I was right;

this is Void's hard drive. Looks like he was hacking into Viacorp."

"Viacorp... they manufacture computer components, right?" I'd heard of them before, of course; it'd be pretty hard not to. But Viacorp was dead quiet compared to some of the other megacorps, with a weak PR presence and very little advertising, at least for the parent company. The only thing most people knew about Viacorp was that no one knew much about them and they liked it that way.

"Way more than that. They also produce prescription medicine, television programming, music... they've got their fingers in a lot of pies," he answered, eyes fixated on the screen before him. "There's a lot of data here. Financial records, order forms, employee rosters, government contracts. It's impressive. For a novice, anyway." I watched him for a moment longer, until he stopped on a chart that looked just like every other. "Whoa, there. What's this?"

"You tell me."

"No need to get snarky. Check out this right here, in the financial records." Wyatt pointed at the screen to a set of numbers. "Looks like Void compiled this on his own. These are the receipts from government contract work. It's mostly regarding the deal a few years back to have Viacorp replace the city's wireless infrastructure."

"I remember that. They still haven't even finished, have they?"

"Nope. And it seems like they never planned to." He clicked a few more times and called up the original contract file. "It's funny, they'd have still made bank even after the costs. City got screwed on this one."

"Hardly unusual." I'd been dealing with unfulfilled promises on the part of the megacorps since they shorted our school supplies back in grade school.

"True, but in most cases, the money stays with the company. However, they bought a ton of Dyscoins worth roughly the same amount that just vanished from the records. They wrote it off as a loss, but Void was able to track them all back to the CEO." I leaned in and he pulled up the personal accounts of one Richard Overton, CEO of Viacorp. All the paperwork showed his personal finances were in shambles, and yet his spending was as extravagant and steady as ever. "I'd be trying to blackmail Overton, but Void was a goody two-shoes, so self righteous. Even if they offered him money, I don't think he would take it."

I recalled Fiona's expensive outfits and her apartment in the Arcology. There was no way he'd be persuaded by money.

"So he was planning to expose him," I said. "That's enough. Thanks for the help, Wyatt. I owe you one."

"I'll be keeping a copy of this data. We'll call it even."

"You better watch it. I hope I won't be investigating your disappearance next." I packed the hard drive up again. "See you around."

The deluge continued, rainwater sweeping the streets clear with its never-ending flow. I was unsure of what to do next; taking the evidence straight to the police wouldn't help me find out what happened to Logan, and they'd probably just sweep it under the rug. If Viacorp was really behind his disappearance, or even just Overton, they'd be sure not to leave any evidence for the police to find. And even if they did, odds are they have the cops on the take, anyway. It wasn't impossible for the police to pursue a corporate case, but it would only be when it was all over the media, and the media would only pick it up if it became too obvious to ignore. That's what Logan had been trying to do, after all. I wasn't too happy with it, either, but I didn't have the resources to do what he couldn't. For a moment, my mind returned to my novels at home, and I wondered again what my heroes would do. Grandpa had never faced a case like this. Sam Spade would visit Overton face-to-face, in the hopes that he'd slip up and provide a clue. With no ideas of my own on how to proceed, it seemed like my best choice was my only choice.

I summoned a cab and prepared for a confrontation during the ride. This could go a number of ways, and I had to be ready, whatever the outcome. The taxi pulled up and I walked into the building, dripping wet. Viacorp's entryway was massive, and almost as cold as the winds outside. It was a clean, sterile sort of place that felt like it had been designed specifically to make visitors uncomfortable. My shoes squeaked with every step across the marble floors, echoing through the deserted lobby until finally I was at the reception desk.

"What can I do for you, sir?" the receptionist asked, the fake smile plastered across her face slowly fading as she noticed my outfit.

"I'm here to see Mister Overton."

"Do you have an appointment? Mister Overton won't see anyone without an appointment."

"I think he'll be willing to make an exception in this case. Tell him I'm here on behalf of the Void. I have a feeling he'll know what I mean." I removed my hat and examined it nonchalantly. The receptionist, quite annoyed at this point, called up to the CEO's office and repeated my message. The low hum of the ventilation system made its presence known during her brief silence.

"Um… oh. Y-yes, sir. I'll send him up right away," she said. She hung up and turned to me. "The executive lift is right behind this desk. Here's a guest code."

I took the ticket from her and entered the elevator. I hung my coat and hat on a hook inside, and tried to clean myself up as I slowly ascended to the top floor. I had just finished straightening my tie when the doors opened. Immediately, two men grabbed me and pulled me into the office. I recognized them from Logan's place the night before. They forced me into a chair in front of the oversized desk in the center of the room.

"Is this any way to treat a guest?" I looked around the room; it was surprisingly spartan, with little to impede the panoramic view of the rain-soaked cityscape, or the Arcology towering over it. Part of the window was covered by the massive letter V of the Viacorp sign outside. Before me was a huge office chair, turned to face the window.

"Let's cut to the chase, shall we, mister...?" Overton said, spinning his chair to face me. I rolled my eyes at his theatrics.

"Canela. Lance Canela," I replied. There wasn't much point in lying if they were able to track down a hacker like Void.

"And what business do you have with me?"

"Oh, I think you know. A missing hacker, public works project, millions of dollars embezzled. Just about everything you're up to at this point," I said. "But I don't care about any of that."

"Is that so?" Overton glared at me, one eyebrow raised. His tailored suit rested evenly upon his shoulders, nearly meeting his dark, slicked back hair.

"I'm only interested in one thing: the location of Logan MacLeod. Show me where he is, and none of this has to get out."

"I'm afraid I have no idea who you're talking about," he replied. There was the faintest hint of a smirk on his face, like a poker player with a bad tell.

"Now who's playing games?" I shook my head. "Perhaps you know him better as the hacker Void."

"Ah, yes. I spoke to him a few weeks back. Quite the self-righteous young fellow, rather disagreeable." Overton's hands came together, fingers intertwined beneath his tightly trimmed beard. "I believe he suffered a rather unfortunate accident not long afterward."

The goons snickered quietly, and I could feel them exchanging glances behind my back. I had a sudden sinking feeling, like I'd made a big mistake coming here.

"The location of his body, then."

"And how can I be sure that you'll honor your word?" he asked. I reached into my left pocket, and the pair stepped forward to stop me. I put up a hand in surrender, then slowly pulled out the hard drive.

"I believe this is what Brawny and Bony over here were searching for last night," I answered. "Turn Logan's body over and you can have it, along with the encryption codes."

"That would be rather difficult; I doubt there's much left of him in the ocean at this point." He was so cavalier that I wondered if Logan wasn't the first. "Now tell me, are you the only one who knows all of this?"

"Yes." No sense dragging Wyatt into this if I could help it.

"I suppose it doesn't matter. I'll have 'Brawny' and 'Bony', as you so whimsically referred to them, follow your tracks. Then perhaps all this ugly business will be behind me once and for all." Overton got up and walked around from behind his desk. My thoughts immediately shifted to Fiona. I tried to stand in protest, but the two men forced me back into the chair. The larger one pulled out a gun, and instantly a claustrophobic sense of panic set in. "I think I'll be calling it a day. Destroy the hard drive, take him away and kill him. Make sure there's no sign he was ever here. I'm afraid that includes the receptionist."

I struggled against them as Overton walked to the elevator, but it was hopeless.

"Whoa, hey now. Wait a minute. Aren't you just supposed to rough me up a little and send me on my way?" I hadn't thought much about the part where Sam Spade gets drugged right after the confrontation.

"I've no reason to take that risk. Farewell, Mister Canela," he called out as the doors closed. Even from behind, I could practically see the smugness on his face.

Brawny and Bony yanked me to my feet. This was my chance; I swept my right leg under Brawny's as I rose from the chair, causing him to fall on his back, hard. His gun went spinning off towards the elevator. I managed to wrestle free from Bony and scrambled across Overton's desk. My heart was pounding; I'd definitely screwed up by coming here. I'm not cut out for this. Desperately, I focused myself. This was no time to be panicking. Panic meant death.

"Just give up. There's no where to run up here," Bony called out in a nasally voice. "Come on out so I don't have to shoot up the boss's desk."

He was right; the only way out was the lift. My pocket weighed heavily on my legs as I crouched up under the desk. Of course—I reached in and pulled out the pistol, a six shot revolver. I didn't have a choice now. I had to fight.

I listened carefully, and heard the sounds of Brawny's heavy footsteps coming around the left side of the desk. I looked out right as he came around the corner and shot him twice at point blank range. It was so loud I could feel it. The first bullet went right into his stomach, but unprepared for the recoil, I fired the second too high. It barely grazed his shoulder and shattered the thick glass behind him, opening the office to the fierce storm outside. We were both caught in a barrage of broken glass, and a stray shard cut my left arm, which started bleeding profusely. Brawny's eyes bulged out as he realized what happened. He fell to his knees, clutching his gut as the wind and rain rushed into the building.

"Johnny!" Bony shouted. I heard the cocking of a gun and dashed to the far side of the desk. Seconds later my prior hiding spot was riddled with bullets. My hands were shaking, but I knew I had to stay in control. Can't afford to miss.

Over the ringing in my ears, I could hear him running over to aid Brawny, so I grit my teeth and stood up. He turned to face me, and I unloaded the remaining bullets as fast as I could. Four deafening explosions rang out, and I couldn't say where they all went. At least one of them struck its target, and he collapsed onto the desk, dropping his gun to the floor. I thought he said something, but I couldn't make it out. I was paralyzed with adrenaline, standing over the two of them. He desperately clawed for the hard drive, but I couldn't force myself to move to stop him. With his last strength, he tossed it meekly towards the opening. Still, it was enough; the drive went careening downward nearly fifty floors. I looked back at him, his eyes conveying the pleasure from one last act of spite before he died.

With my heart racing, I stood in the now vacant room for a moment, listening to the winds whip by. Somehow, I had survived. My hands were still shaking, barely keeping hold of the pistol. I managed to slip it back into my pocket, but it did nothing to calm me down. Looking at the pair, lying in pools of glass and blood, I tried to remind myself that they'd have been all too happy to do the same to me. They were the bad guys here. Thugs, nothing more.

It didn't help.

The executive lift let out a bell sound to announce its return. I stepped inside and rode down, struggling to regain my composure. I took a closer look at my arm; it stung sharply, but it didn't look too deep. I could probably bandage it up myself. As the lift reached ground level, I donned my hat and put on my coat to cover the wound. I nodded to the receptionist on my way out.

Overton was long gone, and the drive had burst into uncountable fragments on the sidewalk, several blocks west due to the wind. This was the real failure; all of Logan's work was lost, and without it there'd be nothing to stop Overton from coming after me, or Fiona, or even Wyatt…

Wyatt! I reached into my trench coat's inner pocket and pulled out my phone to contact him. I noticed I had a message from an unknown number.

"Void was more talented than I gave him credit for. I think he deserves to have this last job." It had been sent only a few minutes ago; it had to be Wyatt. I opened the news app, and was greeted by a headline:

"BREAKING: Viacorp Scandal. Chief Executive Officer's Alleged Embezzlement Scheme Revealed!"

I heaved a sigh in relief. So the hacker has a code of honor after all. Logan's final wish was granted, and his killers had paid the price. Overton would probably flee the country, but either way, he's ruined. Viacorp, trying to minimize the bad PR and maintain privacy, would likely cover up everything else. No one outside the company would ever hear about Brawny and Bony's demise.

I called up a taxi with my phone and headed home. Looking at my arm, it became clear that the hydrophobic coating didn't work quite the same on blood. I only hoped the stain would come out. I bandaged up my arm as well as I could with scraps of gauze and put on a new shirt. It was hard to do the buttons with my hands still shaking. I retrieved the pistol from my pocket and emptied the spent casings. I dropped it into the drawer and slammed it shut. I didn't want to deal with it any more. I just wanted it to be over.

It was then that I realized I had one more grim task ahead of me.

Darkness had fallen once more before Fiona was able to meet with me again. I waited in the booth at the cafe, nursing a sickly sweet beverage as slowly as I could while contemplating just exactly what I was going to tell her. There was no easy way to explain what had become of Logan.

"Mister Canela," she said, walking up. She had a light smile on her face, the glow of hope still present. "I wasn't expecting to hear from you twice in one day."

I stood up and removed my hat, holding it to my chest. "Have a seat."

"Of course." Her expression dulled, and those sparkling green eyes dodged away.

"I don't suppose you've seen the latest news?" I asked, placing my hat on the table as I sat down. Fiona leaned in and shook her head. "Your brother's hacker name was Void. It seems he was trying to expose the corruption in Viacorp, and they caught up with him. I'm sorry, but I wasn't able to locate his final resting place."

Fiona looked down, her hands tightening around the dark blue fabric of her dress. I feared for a moment that she might cry, and I had no idea how I'd deal with that, but it never happened. She looked up, staring straight into my eyes with an iron resolve that I somehow knew her brother had once shared.

"I shouldn't be surprised. It was always a risk, and he knew it."

"I want you to know that the incriminating data that Logan found has been released on the web in his name. The people responsible won't be getting away with this."

Fiona let out a small, relieved laugh. "Thank you, Mister Canela."

Right then, I understood for the first time why Grandpa had been so proud of his work.

# **Sunday**

It was a scorching afternoon in late summer, and I was headed home after another long day without a client. My coat sagged around my shoulders, weighing heavily in that nearly unfamiliar sunlight. The dingy buildings that surrounded my office were dwarfed by most others in the city, but by none more so than the Arcology, the supposedly self-sustaining monolith that made its presence felt all across Kindred. The hopeful connotations of its name belied the reality of the project. A massive hovel in what had become the city's center, it was all but ignored by the police. With a substantial portion of the poorest citizens packed in like sailors on a submarine, it had been almost inevitable.

Of course, it hadn't been a complete failure. The uppermost levels of the Arcology were among the most luxurious and coveted living spaces available, with green parks and clean air. Few places on Earth could better convey how great the gap between the impoverished and the wealthy had become. My apartment was only a few blocks from the western edge, and if business didn't pick up a little I could easily find myself on the other side of the wall.

As I rounded the last corner on my way home, an awful cry pierced through the perpetual din of the city—the kind of anguished, inhuman sound that only a human can make. I looked around until I spotted the source: an old woman, screaming at the top of her lungs as she hustled down the street.

I picked up my pace and ran towards her. She wasn't being chased, so far as I could tell, but her tattered clothes led me to believe she had good reason to hurry.

"My daughter! Someone has to help her. It's been days…" she stopped to catch her breath for a moment, leaning on her knees. I reached her not long afterward, and she looked up at me with lively blue eyes that were fraught with concern. "Please, she's all I have left."

"Are you okay? What happened?" I asked, leaning down to her eye level. She wheezed loudly, unable to look up. "Just take a moment to catch your breath and tell me what's going on."

It was about then that a police car rolled around the far corner. The woman took off again, gasping for air between each step. I tried to follow her, but she didn't get far before the cops cut her off. I skidded to a halt and watched as the officers emerged.

"Get back! You're useless. I need real help," she shouted at them, stumbling back a little bit before falling. The closer officer caught up and tried to drag her to her feet. "You should be ashamed. You don't stand for justice, you're just thugs."

"Ma'am, we're just taking you back to the Arcology. It's illegal to cross into the outer city. If you need to leave, file for a temporary leave permit and go through the checkpoints like everyone else," one of the cops said as his partner wrestled with her. She was putting up an admirable struggle until he yanked her arms hard behind her back, and she cried out in pain. I wanted to rush over and help, but I knew it would only make things worse. Both cops grabbed her bodily, and together were able to toss her in the back seat with little effort. For an instant, our eyes made contact, and I could feel the fear and hopelessness pouring out of her.

"Ugh, what a pain in the ass. This is going to be so much paperwork," the first cop said, walking around to the driver's side. His partner sighed in agreement.

"She's lucky we didn't just taze her. Maybe that's what we

should do next time," he replied. They both laughed and climbed into the car. I walked over to engage them, but they drove off and disappeared behind the same corner from which they had emerged. I stared at the empty road for a moment, trying to take in what I'd just seen. It was rare for anyone to make it through the Arcology's border security, much less someone as frail as that poor woman had been. If she'd felt her only option was committing what had essentially been a jailbreak, it must be serious. I sighed and shook my head, then resumed the walk home.

The scene played through my head the rest of the night. The old woman's face was chiseled into my memory: curled hair that had lost its color long ago, resting just above tired brown eyes. She had stopped fighting once the doors were closed, despair overtaking panic. The lines on her face from decades of senseless labor had sunk to their natural crestfallen position. It was the face of someone who had long ago become accustomed to a life of resignation and failure, a haunting expression that kept me tossing and turning until the sun came up.

By the time my alarm went off in the morning, I hadn't slept a wink. I hated that sound, but I had no way to know otherwise; the Arcology blocked the sun in my part of the city until just after noon, on those rare occasions when it was out at all. I got dressed in the dim room, complete with trench coat and hat, and grabbed a stale bagel on my way out the door. As I headed to the office, my phone chirped with the reminders of unpaid bills. I silenced it and looked back over my shoulder at the massive structure looming over me. The old woman's cries rang through my head one more time.

I tried to ignore the needling voice in the back of my mind. I couldn't just go in there. I don't know her name, or where she lives. There are tens of thousands of people living on the first floor alone; I'd never find her by chance. Besides, I needed to be available in case a paying client came in.

But each step grew more and more difficult, until finally I came to a halt with a sigh. If I were actually going to do this, I'd need papers to pass through the Arcology checkpoints, and I'd need more information to track her down. I had a contact who might be able to help with both of those, so I called up a taxi and programmed in a destination that I often hoped to avoid: the police department.

The law enforcement of Kindred was always frustrating to deal with. Corruption had run rampant in recent years, with the advent of laws granting the police new and extreme powers only compounding the issue. The few remaining cops who were on the level were overworked and underpaid, and completely unwilling to speak out against their less savory colleagues. Their reasons varied, but be it out of fear or just that old blue code of silence, the end result was a police force with the fire power of a military run by the kind of men I wouldn't trust with a pellet gun. I only interacted with them as much as my job required, but through a few cases I'd managed to become friendly with Sergeant Solomon McKinney, probably the most upstanding man left in the department. If anyone could help me get in there, it would be him.

I made my way to his precinct and found the place as crowded and bustling as usual. The building had an outdated, 1970s-style appearance, hidden under a thick veneer of filth in the eight decades since. Convicts were brought in and marched out frequently, keeping the for-profit prisons outside the city well stocked and lucrative. Half the cops were on the take from organized crime and half from the megacorp jailers, so it was a pretty nice racket if you didn't mind ruining some kid's future. I cautiously approached the desk and got the receptionist's attention.

"If you're looking for the courthouse, it's two blocks east of here," he said without looking up from his tablet.

"Actually, I'm looking for Sergeant McKinney. Is he available?"

He gazed up at me with an expression somewhere between apathy and disgust.

"No, he's pretty tied up at the moment." His eyes immediately flitted back down to the screen. "Lotta paperwork."

"I'll only be a minute. Can you just tell him that Lance Canela would like to speak to him?"

"...Fine." He tapped the tablet's screen a few times, then waited. In a few seconds, the device rang out with a ding sound that was barely audible over the noise of the lobby. "Go on back."

I glared at him disapprovingly, but the man didn't notice. I headed through the crowded rows of desks to Solomon's office. Behind the scratched and beaten wood divider sat a middle-aged man staring blankly at a tablet. I knocked on the door's glass as I entered the room.

"Good morning, Sergeant." He glanced up, and he looked so much more tired than the last time we'd met—deep set eyes with the circles of many a sleepless night surrounding them. He'd grown thin and gaunt, and his once jet-black hair had taken on a silver frost. You'd never guess he wasn't much older than I was.

"Isn't it a little warm for that coat?" McKinney asked, searching the surface of his desk.

"It's never too warm for this coat." I looked down at its weathered fabric, worn for longer than I'd been alive.

"Suit yourself," he said, shuffling through the drawers of a desk that looked older than he was. "It's great to see you and all, but now's not the best time. There've been some reports of trespassers at the top of the Arcology and now I've got this jurisdictional nightmare to deal with."

"I'm actually here for a similar matter. Did you get any reports about a woman who crossed the Arcology border into the city? She was detained pretty quickly."

"I think I saw that earlier. Give me a second." He picked up the tablet that had been resting precariously on the corner of the desk, swiping and tapping it a few times. "Yeah, here it is. Says it was an old woman named… Laverne Warner. Beats the hell out of me how she got through that fence. Doesn't look like she was in any shape to climb it."

"Mind telling me what happened to her?"

"She claims that her daughter was abducted, but you know what the Arcology's base is like. We weren't even able to confirm whether or not she actually had a child. After that, she refused to communicate any further, so she was returned to the Arcology with a penalty on record." He skimmed the report, then looked up, staring me down. "Your turn: why are you interested in this?"

"I happened to see her in the city and was hoping she might trust someone who wasn't a cop. Would you be able to do me a favor and help me get in there to meet with her?"

"How about you do yourself a favor, Lance, and don't get involved. This lady ain't going to be paying anyone for their services, I can tell you that right now."

"I'm just curious, that's all. If you can get me a checkpoint pass for a week or so, that ought to be enough."

"You know she's probably just some senile old loon, rambling every crazy thought that comes to mind."

"Then, our short meeting today aside, the only person whose time I've wasted will be my own."

Raised eyebrows turned his stare incredulous. I was dead set on this, however, and he knew it. He could throw me out, if he really wanted, but that wouldn't solve the problem. At this point, it'd be easier to humor me, and he knew that, too. He sighed with resignation and placed his hands on the table.

"I always knew you were an idealistic son of a bitch. Sometimes I envy that. Then I remember that kind of thing'll get you killed." McKinney stood up, and set the tablet down on the corner once more. "Look, I'll see what I can do."

He shuffled out of the office, looking for someone who could get a pass authorized. I leaned forward and picked up his tablet. I memorized her name and address as quickly as possible, then carefully set it back where it had been. Not long afterward, McKinney returned and pulled up a permit file on the tablet. I held out my phone, but he hesitated.

"Don't make me regret this. I have enough to deal with without you adding to it."

"I promise, I'll handle it myself." He sighed, and finally transferred the pass.

"You've got five days. Good luck."

# Monday

I left the station and headed back home to prepare. I wouldn't be able to take much in with me, but I felt I should be ready to defend myself. Shuffling through my nightstand drawer, I found my pistol laying inside, locked. I hadn't been able to bring myself to touch it since the incident at Viacorp; even looking at it caused nothing but a flood of intense memories to come back. Grandpa had once tried to tell me that the cost of firing in self-defense was far greater than just the price of the rounds in the gun, but I was too young to listen back then. A few months ago I'd found it scribbled down on one of the blank pages in the back of *The Long Goodbye*, a warning across time that had arrived just a little too late. Only then did I finally understand. The thought of having to use it again was a repulsive one, but if it came down to it, what choice would I have? I convinced myself that if he could live with it, then so could I. Or at least, I repeated it until I thought I was convinced.

With the gun safely stashed away, I set out towards the western gate of the Arcology, not far from where I'd seen the old woman the day before. I tried to remind myself that this could be a dangerous trip; muggings, despite the fact that few people carried physical currency these days, were extremely common. Gang violence had become so prevalent in certain areas of the structure that the police department had simply stopped reporting it altogether in the city's crime statistics. While there were cops assigned here, it was generally viewed as a form of punishment for those who refused to go along with the status quo. Facing the worst of humanity all cooped up together, it didn't take long for any notions of justice or righteousness to get beaten out of them. Rumor had it that when quota time came around, they simply rounded up random people off the street, inevitably guilty of something, and made up the case against them afterward. I always hoped it was exaggerated, that things couldn't actually be so bad. Guess I'll find out soon enough.

For some reason, I had expected a line, but there were only one or two people trying to cross into the Arcology. Most people didn't visit unless they had to. I hid my pistol carefully and stepped into the checkpoint. Two guards approached immediately and asked for my papers. I handed them my phone, with the permit I'd received from Sergeant McKinney on screen, and waited in silence as they reviewed it. One of them took it into the guardhouse for a moment, and the other walked up to me, standing so close I could feel the warmth of his breath on my face.

"What business do you have here?" he asked, staring me in the eye.

"Just doing a bit of investigation for a client. Can't talk too much about it," I answered, leaning back a bit. It technically wasn't a lie, after all. His judgmental stare continued until the other guard came out of the shack.

"It checks out. You may enter the Arcology until Friday at nine PM."

"Thank you." I backed away and nodded to the more distant of the pair. I went through my pockets, handing over anything he decided was contraband.

"Here's a respirator. You are to wear it at all times when outdoors. Be sure to keep an eye on any personal possessions you choose to take with you. The pickpockets in there are pretty sly, and you will be held responsible for any problems caused by items lost inside," he said. Then, as I passed, "Oh, and you can leave that here, too."

"Understood," I replied, slowly retrieving the gun. Honestly, I was a little relieved that I'd no longer have to worry about whether to use it. I handed it over as the first set of gates in the checkpoint slid open. I stepped inside the sally port and put on the respirator as I waited for one set of doors to close and the next to open.

Even though I'd always known this side of the city existed, seeing it was a different experience. The air was thick with fumes and dust, and the sky dark, blotted out by the soot-stained bottom of the next floor. Only a sliver of sunlight broke through the wide openings at the top of the walls this time of day, giving the whole place an atmosphere of eternal night. The grid-like streets of the Arcology were illuminated by regularly placed streetlights, each with a barely noticeable camera underneath, standing watch for as far as the eye could see. Some of the buildings predated the Arcology's construction, and it wasn't hard to pick them out at a glance. Busted and boarded up windows, walls caked with grime and pollution that could do little besides settle on the concrete surfaces all around. Cars had been banned down here only a few years ago, but it was hardly an issue by then; if you had to live here, you couldn't afford one anyway. Automated streetcars had once been installed, but they became excellent targets for holdups, and were eventually shut down. Bare metal rails were all that remained.

The streets running east to west were lettered, and those running north to south numbered, making it a simple matter to locate a particular address. I was looking for the corner of M-22, which wasn't very far from the checkpoint. As I walked down the cracked and broken asphalt, I tried to keep my eyes from wandering across the cityscape. There was little doubt in my mind that outsiders would be unwelcome here, and gawking at my surroundings would effectively put a target on my back. I kept my hat low and eyes to the ground, always listening and trying to remain aware of nearby activity. Skittering sounds came from the alleys, and the occasional bold rat dashed from one side of the street to the other. People outside were few and far between; those who were clearly had no other choice, mostly the drugged up and the homeless. At least here, they didn't have to worry about the frequent rain.

As I came up to the intersection, I took special care to reinforce the appearance that I knew where I was going. A few concrete walls had the faintest signs of graffiti buried under the dirt to help differentiate one building from the next. Spotting a broken address sign, I climbed the stairs and heaved open the thick metal door. There was no lobby, no ornamentation; just plain, simple halls broken only by evenly spaced faux wooden doors, which stood out largely because of how unsuitable their natural appearance was in the manufactured monochrome of the Arcology. Halfway down, I found the door with a label matching the one I'd seen in McKinney's files.

I removed the respirator as I stood in front of her door. Maybe McKinney is right, and she really is just a senile old loon. Too late to turn back now. A muffled rapping sound echoed down the halls with each knock.

"Go away. I'm not expecting anyone and I've had enough trouble lately," an old voice called out. Frail, but with a kind of intensity that let you know this lady was no longer going to be putting up with any bullshit.

"Ah, yes, ma'am, I'm sorry to disturb you, but—"

"Then don't."

"I saw you outside the Arcology."

Locks briefly scraped together before the door opened just a sliver. That same wrinkled face, so clearly etched in my memory from the day before, peaked one suspicious eye out at me.

"Well, you sure don't look like you're from around here," she said, her eye looking me up and down. "Wait, you were there when those brutes caught me, weren't you?"

"Indeed. My name is Lance Canela, and I'm a private detective. May I come in and speak to you for a moment?"

"You certainly look the part... alright, but only because this is so important." Mrs. Warner opened the door wide enough for me to enter, then slammed it shut and locked it. I removed my hat and looked around the tiny flat, which had a stark emptiness to it that only enhanced the chill in the air, reminiscent of an underground bunker. Four recessed ceiling lights provided the only illumination, shining their harsh blue tones down onto the meager furniture spread throughout the room. A tiny kitchenette and what I could only hope was the bedroom were off to the side.

"Well, have a seat. I don't have anything to offer you, sorry. Water rationing is pretty tight this time of year," she said, gesturing towards the threadbare sofa as she crept around a scratched coffee table to a chair on the other side. I noticed her left wrist was covered in dark, ugly bruises, colored a sickly mixture of black and yellow. She was lucky, if that was the worst she got.

"That's quite alright. I'd like to get right down to business, if you don't mind," I answered, sitting down carefully.

"Right, time is of the essence. Who knows what's happened to her already."

"Could you start from the beginning for me? What had you so concerned that you'd risk crossing into the city?"

She heaved a sigh, the kind that only someone already resigned to the next in a long chain of hardships could muster. She stared at the table for a moment before looking up at me with that resolve I'd seen the day before.

"My daughter, Melanie, disappeared about a week ago. I haven't been able to find any sign of her, not even a note. Someone has to have taken her." She let out an empty, wistful laugh that rang hollow with bitterness. "Probably lured her in with a little cash. I told her not to bother herself over my problems, but she just wouldn't take that for an answer."

"Seems she shares a bit of your tenacity." I sat up straight. "Can you tell me what kind of problems you're facing?"

"Oh, just what you'd expect an old woman to be dealing with. My health's been on the decline... getting around isn't as easy as it used to be, but that's life. People lived worse than this in the past, so I've got no right to complain."

"It sounds like you're getting by." I glanced around the barren room, looking for anything that might help. The only personal belongings were a pair of old photos on the wall. The first was an aged professional photo of a well-dressed couple, which I assumed to be Laverne and her husband. The other was a small picture of a young girl, wearing what appeared to be a more tattered version of Laverne's dress from the first, standing out of focus with a nervous smile on her face. "Is that Melanie?"

"What?" she asked, looking around. I pointed to the photograph on the wall. "Oh! Yes, that's her. We took that picture about ten years ago. Teddy and I lost everything in the post-war recession right before she was born. We couldn't give Melanie much growing up, so that picture's one of the only mementos from her childhood. It made our struggles a little more worthwhile, just to see her so happy for a day. We'd have done anything for our little girl."

"Maybe she's trying to do the same for you now. Is there any reason she might have chosen now to leave on her own? Did anything happen recently to spur her into action?"

"Well... I had an appointment at the free clinic about a month ago. It's hard to get over there, but I wouldn't dare miss it. The waitlists can be so absurd, you know. She made sure I got there, but the doctor told me that I have early-stage lung cancer. The clinic can't do much about that."

"I—I'm sorry to hear that." What else could be said when

someone you've just met tells you that?

"I don't mean to lay it on you like that. It's inevitable, with the air like it is down here. But I have no regrets; there've been hard times, but I'm content with the life I've led. Melanie, however… nobody takes that kind of news about their parents well."

"Perhaps she's earning money for your treatment."

"If that were the case, why not tell me? Why run off like this?" she asked, her voice laced with an earnest sense of confusion. It had clearly never occurred to her that her daughter might do something illegal to earn cash, and I wasn't about to break it to her. I decided to try a different tactic.

"Do you know if she had any friends, anyone that might know more about what she was up to?"

"There was a boy… I only met him a few times, but he seemed nice. What was his name again?" Laverne raised a hand to her face and rubbed the temples of her worn and wrinkled face. "Barry? No… Cheren? No, Darren! Yes, that's it. Darren Meyers. I think they met because he works at the food bank for this sector."

"Thanks for the info. I'll go talk to him right away," I said. I rose to my feet and offered a hand. She accepted, lifting herself up in a deliberate manner. "I'll do everything I can to find Melanie for you."

"I have to tell you now, don't be expecting I can pay you for your services."

"It's alright, ma'am. A pro bono case is good every once in a while." I picked up my hat and put the respirator back on as I left.

I walked down the deserted hall, staring at the ground. Odds were that Melanie had gotten herself wrapped up in something illegal and paid for it with her life. There weren't many ways to earn money in the depths of the Arcology, and almost all of them were criminal. Drug dealing and smuggling, gambling, larceny… she'd never be accepted for a maintenance job, and anything else would involve crossing into the city at large. I hoped that somehow I'd find some better news to bring the old woman.

I'd known it would be a bad idea to bring much of value in here, but I was wishing I'd at least brought a map. All the streets looked the same, row after row of identical gray buildings varying only in the damage they'd taken over the years. The looming, darkened forms of the Arcology's outer walls gave the whole area an unsettling atmosphere that left me on edge. Occasionally, I'd pass an unconscious man in worn out clothes lying in an alleyway, or a feral dog picking through an overturned dumpster, which served as the closest things to landmarks this place had.

I managed to locate the food bank, a one-story structure with a busted plastic sign at the corner of R and 18. According to the hours listed on the door it'd be closing soon, and the vacant lobby agreed. The small front desk was unmanned, and offered only a tarnished silver bell as proof that the store was still in use. I rang it once, and waited for a moment. Eventually, a tired young man who looked to be in his mid-twenties emerged from the loosely hanging curtain to the backroom.

"We're closing in a few minutes. You'll have to come back tomorrow," he said, as if by rote. His dark hair was unkempt, and he'd gone several weeks without shaving. The bags under his eyes were so dark I wondered if he'd ever slept.

"Actually, I was hoping to speak to Darren. Is he available?" I asked. The man raised his guard instantly.

"Depends on who's asking."

"The name's Lance Canela." I removed the mask once again and offered a hand. He eyed me suspiciously, no doubt trying to judge my motivations. "I came here in regards to Melanie Warner; I was told he was acquainted with her."

"You a cop?"

"No, not now or ever. I'm a private detective working on her mother's behalf." This seemed to satisfy him, and he relaxed a bit, leaning forward onto the chipped and worn counter.

"Alright, I'll buy that for now. Can't be too careful, after all. Not doing anything wrong, but that hardly matters these days."

"Unfortunately," I agreed. "So you're Darren?"

"Yeah."

"And you do know Melanie Warner?"

"Have for a while now."

"When was the last time you saw her?"

"Ah, a little over a week ago, the Saturday before last. She was… over at my place," he said.

"Are you aware that she hasn't been home in almost as long?"

"That's kinda unusual, but nothing to worry about yet." His voice was steady, but the slight trembling of his eyes betrayed him.

"Did she show any odd behavior? Any sign that she might be leaving?" I asked. Darren stood up straight and lifted the counter's divider, beckoning me to follow him into the back. He began moving around boxes of synthetic meat as if out of nervous habit.

"Look, I'm only telling you this cause I'm worried, too. But there's not a lot I can do down here. You're from the outside, right?"

"I am."

"Alright," he sighed, and checked around one last time. Roaches scattered from the hard fluorescent light as he hoisted another box off the floor. "She said something like that, yeah. Some kind of an agency or whatever, that said they could hook her up with a job. Sounded sketchy to me. I told her that."

"From what I know of the Arcology, it definitely sounds suspicious. Do you know the name of the agency? Any other details that might help?"

"Ascended Employment? Something like that. I'd never heard of it, and believe me, I know every kind of legal job there is down here. That's why I'm doing this for free. Couldn't find anything better."

I nodded in agreement. I had to admire his dedication to his principles; it wouldn't be easy to stay honest, living in this permanent underworld. He stopped moving boxes for a moment and looked me in the eye for the first time.

"Please, find her. I'd hate for something bad to happen to her, but she's always so stubborn. It's near impossible to talk her out of something once she's made up her mind. If there's any way I can help, just come find me. I'm almost always here."

"Thanks, Darren. I'll keep that in mind." I shook his hand firmly. "I'll do my best to get her back for you."

I put my hat and mask back on as I stepped outside once again. It was that narrow time of day when the sun was angled just so, the one point every afternoon where the denizens of the Arcology could catch sight of it. A gunshot echoed down the empty concrete streets, and I ducked behind the building until I was sure the culprits weren't heading my way. I took it as my cue to head home.

As I made my way back to the exit at N-26, I went over the case. A sickly mother, a rare job opportunity, a concerned boyfriend. Ascended Employment Agency. Something told me that hitting the streets wouldn't be the way to find information on a group that even a resident like Darren had never heard of. There was only one person that could find the answers I needed with time to spare. When I got home, I fired off an encrypted message and went to bed.

# **Tuesday**

As I wandered out of my bedroom early the next morning, it occurred to me that my apartment really wasn't much bigger than Mrs. Warner's. I guess things aren't so different outside of the Arcology after all. I tossed on my coat and hat and walked outside just in time to catch a taxi.

The skies were smoothed over in a uniform ash gray, as if mirroring the concrete surfaces of the city below. I was on my way to see Wyatt, a contact I'd known for well over a year now. Wyatt was a hacker who went by the name of Sigil, and I'd found he was willing to do a little technological legwork if there was something in it for him. Fortunately for me, a bit of entertainment was often enough to get him to take a look.

The taxi came to a halt in a familiar section of downtown, near a rundown pub with a sign that had fallen some months ago. The bartender looked up from his tablet as I entered. I gestured toward the back, and he grunted before returning his attention to the device. I climbed the dark staircase tucked away in the rear and knocked on the door at the top. To my surprise, locks scratched and turned, and it swung open, revealing the bulbous figure on the other side. A loose T-shirt hung on his frame like a tent, struggling to hide his corpulent belly. His shaggy brown hair was faintly rimmed by the bluish glow of a half-dozen computer monitors.

"Good morning, Wyatt. I take it this company was a little more interesting than I expected." He winced at the mention of his name, then sat back down in his top of the line office chair. I closed the door behind me.

"I gotta say, Lance, I was pretty annoyed when I first saw that message. Can't do your own internet searches?" He turned on his augmented reality goggles, settled himself in and began opening a few files.

"I had good reason to believe that there wasn't going to be a lot of info on the upper levels of the net."

"Yeah, well, you were right. There was almost nothing."

"Almost, huh?" I asked, leaning in to look at his low screen. "Don't keep me in suspense."

"Well, well. Isn't this unusual?" he smirked. If there was one thing Wyatt loved, it was having the upper hand.

"I'm on a time limit here. Cut to the chase."

"Why are you always in such a hurry? I know you're not that busy. Definitely not busier than me." Wyatt pulled up an image on the screen. "Anyway, here. All I could find were a handful of social media posts from about three months back. It looks like a bunch of rich kids joking around, but then all the posts were deleted two days later."

He waved his hand and the file appeared on my phone. The opening post was a complaint about a butler refusing to follow some kind of ridiculous orders and quitting over it. The first few replies were sympathetic and just as self-absorbed, before someone suggested he hire his next staff from Ascended Employment. There were one or two replies of confusion, ending with a request for more information from the original poster.

"It was deleted after this?"

"Yeah. The thing is, that's the only mention on the mainstream internet at all. I've tried poking around the deep web and that name still doesn't provide any results."

"So there's no way that's a legitimate company. It's impossible to do business without a web presence."

"Of course. But that's not just true of legitimate companies; even criminal organizations make use of corporate-style PR tactics these days. Whatever this group does—if it really exists— has to be pretty serious to keep it this quiet." He swiveled around and looked up at me, brown eyes hidden behind a digital veil. A devilish smile crept across his face. "I bet they'd be willing to pay a lot of money to make sure it stays that way, too."

"Hey, now. This could be a matter of life and death. You can't extort them or anything, at least not until I can figure out what's up."

Wyatt snorted, the grin melting away into an expression of surly displeasure.

"Fine, but when you do finish this up, leave something for me."

"I'll see what I can do," I said, but I wasn't really interested in helping him perform blackmail, secret or not. "I think I know what to do now. Thanks for the help, Wyatt."

"You owe me one. And I told you to call me Sigil!" he shouted after me. It seemed like the only way to find out more about Ascended would be to find one of these rich families in contact with them and get closer that way. That would be tricky, however; many of the city's richest residents lived in Magmell, that uppermost block of the Arcology that had become their stronghold. While you could get a legal pass to travel into the lower areas of the Arcology from the police or the city government, travel to that lofty realm was strictly by invitation. Even public servants and maintenance crews were closely watched and escorted for the duration of their work. If I wanted to do any investigating up there, I'd need someone who lived there to let me in.

I stepped into my office for the first time in a few days. The door was still locked, the shelves untouched; there was no sign that anyone had visited in the meantime. The phone chirped its bill reminders again, as if to rub it in.

Sitting down at the desk, I kicked on the computer and started to search for some of these names. I was able to find their profiles easily enough, but they looked pretty normal. Self-taken photos of two or three of them at a time, dressed in expensive clothes and so clearly drunk that the photo likely served as the only memory any of them had of that night. Posts congratulating each other on how much fun they'd had and how great the next night or weekend would be. They had no worries, no bills chirping demands at them. Just an endless life of partying. Must be nice.

All of the people from Wyatt's list were marked as friends, and the multitude of pictures they had of each other made it clear it was more than a digital illusion. The group had one more member, however—a man in the pictures named Jake Freely who hadn't commented on the Ascended posting. I checked out his profile: mid-twenties, clearly the youngest of the group. He seemed to be a new arrival, only just moved into Magmell in the last two years. He had no family listed, but it didn't take much effort to figure out that his father was an upper level executive at Gyrospec and probably made more in a week than I would in my whole life. But then again, that was minimum requirements for living up there.

It was clear at this point that I'd made it as far as I could searching online. If I wanted to progress any further, I'd need to get into Magmell. I wracked my brain for a while, trying to find an in, when it finally came to me: Fiona. She'd been quite grateful for my services in spite of the outcome, so with any luck I might be able to convince her to let me look around for a few hours.

I rummaged through my computer's old case files in search of Fiona's contact info, making a mental note to organize them better the next time I had a chance. There was a special extension needed to get through to phones in Magmell, and the phone network filtered out any calls from the rest of Kindred unless an exception was listed. Naturally, this didn't apply to the business district downtown; only to the plebes of the city at large. I just had to hope I was still an exception.

I leaned back in my chair, feet kicked up on the desk. The phone rang three times before a sultry voice came across the line.

"Hello? May I ask who's calling?" she asked, a note of surprise in her voice. Unexpected calls had to be an alien concept for her.

"Good morning, Miss MacLeod. This is Lance Canela. I'm the private detective you hired a few months ago." There, good start. Investigating the slums was a cakewalk compared to having to ask a favor.

"Ah, right! Mister Canela. Yes." Fiona breathed a sigh of relief. "It's good to hear from you again. Is there something I can help you with?" She sounded so sweet, as if legitimately excited to hear from me once more. I took it as a good sign.

"Indeed. I've got a favor to ask of you, if you wouldn't mind." A metallic clank rang out, and I realized I was fiddling with a drawer handle. I leaned back until it was out of reach and glanced out between the venetian blinds. The streets were pretty empty at this time of day; only cracked sidewalks and stagnant puddles waited outside the club now. The sky had only grown darker since I'd left Wyatt's hideout.

"Go on."

"Yes… well, you see, my latest case has given me cause to investigate the upper levels of the Arcology, but it's not easy to get up there," I said. The blinds snapped shut, and I sat up.

"You'd like for me to invite you up, then?"

"Yes, ma'am. That would be extremely helpful. We don't even have to actually see each other; I just need a few hours to poke around, look for clues. That sort of thing."

"That shouldn't be a problem," Fiona said. "I'll send an aerocar to pick you up on one condition."

"What's that?" I pulled my chair up closer to the desk, but caught myself before I could touch the handle again.

"Let's have lunch together when you arrive."

I was taken aback, but agreed wholeheartedly to the suggestion. She gave me some instructions as to when and how I could locate the aerocar when it arrived.

"Thank you, Miss MacLeod. I'll set off right away."

"I told you, it's nothing. And please, call me Fiona."

"Alright. Goodbye, Fiona."

"Goodbye."

Excellent. Keep it together; remain professional. Philip Marlowe wouldn't get worked up over that. I tossed my hat back on and went out to hail another taxi.

With Magmell so isolated from the rest of the city, travel to and from wasn't easy. Many of the residents owned or rented access to aerocars, a heavily regulated mode of transportation. Few of the residents could (legally) operate one themselves, so the drivers were among the few lower-class citizens able to gain access to that area. With so many different clients, the driver just might have some useful information himself.

I got out at the Michael G. Arin terminal, the only port for aerocars nestled in the heart of the business district. I felt extremely out of place here since, with exception of the staff, every person I could see was decked out in designer clothes or finely tailored business suits. My weather-beaten trench coat garnered many a stare as I made my way to the boarding room Fiona had described. The installation was quite classy, with uniquely handcrafted chandeliers spaced evenly down the halls, and terminals featuring the finest leather sofas you could find. Heavy mahogany doors lined the path, each one leading to a hangar of vehicles that could easily cost half a million each. A statue of the port's namesake dominated the atrium at the end of the hall. Golden adornments surrounded the marble entrepreneur like offerings at an ancient shrine, a monument to wealth's ability to generate more wealth. Such is the world of business.

I spotted the driver in the terminal, holding a pad with my name on it. He was decked out in a full chauffeur's uniform, sandy blonde hair just visible under the rim of his hat.

"I'm Lance. I take it you're Miss MacLeod's driver?" It seemed a little redundant, but I felt obligated to ask. I expected a look of disgust, but instead was greeted with a sigh of relief.

"Yes, sir. Shall we get underway?"

"Yeah. Let's go," I replied, and he led the way outside to the ruby red aerocar, a close match for Fiona's hair. It was quite a beauty: without wheels, the fluid, aerodynamic curves of a sports car could continue around the entire body unimpeded, giving it an elegantly feminine look. Powerful ducted fans extended out from the sides where wheels would ordinarily be, surrounding a narrow passenger compartment just large enough for four people, paired up and facing each other. The driver was nearly isolated, centered in the front of the craft, as opposed to offset to one side like an ordinary car. I climbed into the back and we took off.

"So, what brings you to Magmell? You don't really look like my typical clientele, if you don't mind me saying so," he said as soon as we were in the air.

"Nah, you're right. I'm a private detective meeting with Miss MacLeod as part of an investigation." I figured honesty would be the best way to gain his trust.

"Oh yeah? What're you investigating? If you can talk about it, that is."

"I'm looking into this company called Ascended Employment. Ever heard of it?" I watched for some sign of reaction from him, but he was nearly impossible to read from this angle.

"Hmm… can't say I have. It doesn't sound like something you'd find in the upper levels, though. Not many people looking for jobs."

"True enough," I replied. If he had no information, there wasn't much reason to explain further. "Just a rumor, that's all."

"Ah, I see. Well, if I do hear something about it I'll be sure to let you know."

"Thanks." There was something about his tone that I couldn't quite place, but I decided to let it go. The conversation turned to the grim weather brewing, and from there to other forms of small talk until we arrived. I got out onto a landing pad atop Fiona's building and tried to give the man a tip, but he politely yet firmly declined, stating that Fiona had already taken care of everything. The driver took off shortly afterward, returning the vehicle to the terminal on this end.

The clouds were so much closer up here, their flat, gray bases forming an impenetrable ceiling that kept the city dark. The air was noticeably cooler and thinner than it had been at the surface, leaving me a bit lightheaded. I looked out across the entire level. Fiona's apartment was on the outer ring, which doubled as a shield for the fierce winds that could flare up at this altitude. The inner radius contained a number of large mansions, reserved for the most rich and powerful members of the city's elite. Each one had a substantial lawn, immaculately landscaped and strewn with every symbol of wealth one could think of—fountains, statues, topiaries, exotic plants. The works. Nothing like the endless rows of concrete slabs down below. The middle of the level appeared to be a public garden, with an ornate fountain as the centerpiece, built up to disguise the ugly utilitarian nature of the central support. However much wealth Fiona might have, it was nothing compared to the fortunes amassed by her neighbors.

"Mister Canela!" a familiar voice called out. I turned around and saw a curvaceous red-headed figure standing in the door of the building. She was wearing a navy dress with a collar and trim that were sparkling white. Just above the modest neckline was a tight pearl necklace, barely visible. I walked up and greeted her.

"It's good to see you again, Fiona," I said. "Although, it seems like if I am to use your first name, it would be better for it to go both ways, wouldn't it?

"I suppose it would." She smiled, a tiny gesture that momentarily eased my nerves. "Lance."

"You're looking well."

"I've been getting by. And you?"

"Oh, the same."

"Right." She nodded. The winds whistled by, whipping the tail of my coat around wildly. "Shall we head inside? It can get pretty nasty out here in a storm."

"Lead the way." I gestured down the hall, and she headed off to her apartment.

Dim sconces lined the hall, their light softly bouncing off cream-colored walls. The carpeted floors absorbed our footsteps, giving the hall an oppressive sense of stillness.

"I see you took the time to check the weather before heading up here," she said. I looked over, confused. "The coat. Aren't you wearing it in case it rains?"

"This? No, I just wear it all the time."

A panel recognized her as we approached, and the door slid open. Her apartment was huge, and had a delightful floral scent to it, light but certainly noticeable. The walls in the main room were covered in a soft, patterned wallpaper. She led the way into the dining room, which featured an antique table set with carvings so finely detailed it could only be described as a work of art. The food on the table, by contrast, was rather simple, with fresh salads set out and a selection of sandwich ingredients to choose from.

"Nice place."

"Thank you. I'm a little embarrassed by how ostentatious it must look to you. A lot of these things belonged to my grandparents, and they're a bit showy for my tastes," she said, pointing me to a chair. "Please, have a seat."

I sat down, and she did the same soon afterward. I looked at the spread laid out before us, and that anxious feeling returned.

"Well, everything certainly looks great," I said, struggling to keep the conversation going. "Wait, are these… real vegetables?"

"Yes, actually. They're from the farming levels," she replied. It had been a long time since I'd seen food like this, freshly picked by machines right here in the heart of the city. I marveled at it for a moment in place of actually speaking up. The silence stretched out until finally, "Lance, it's okay. You don't have to be nervous. I asked you here, remember?"

"Yeah, right. Sorry." I wasn't sure exactly what I'd been doing to give it away, but I tried to push it aside and act normal.

"That is what you wanted me to call you, isn't it?"

"Oh, yeah. That's fine." I nodded and tried to take a bite. I wasn't really sure how you were supposed to eat salad, so I could only hope I wasn't embarrassing myself further.

"Good. So, why don't tell me about this case that's led us to meet once again?"

I explained to her about Melanie, and Ascended Employment. I told her about the posts Wyatt had shown me. And somehow, talking about the case, I didn't feel so nervous any more. Fiona listened attentively, but waited until I was finished to speak up.

"I see. Well, I can't say that I've heard of Ascended Employment, and I don't think you'd get very far wandering around up here unattended."

I sighed, trying to hide my disappointment. Back to square one. "It's okay. I should have known the security up here would be tight. I'll head home and hit the streets for a new lead in the morning."

"Hey now, wait a minute. It's not all lost yet," Fiona placed a hand on mine as I stood up to leave. I paused.

"You've just told me I won't be able to do much sleuthing up here, and that was my only hope for this. I need to go back and find another lead," I said, but one look into those deep green eyes told me right where this conversation was headed.

"Not exactly. I said you won't be able to look around unattended." She stared back at me, and a glimmer of excitement crossed her face. "So I'll escort you around."

"Forget it. It's too dangerous. You have no idea the kind of trouble I ran into while investigating your brother." The firefight at the top of Viacorp flashed through my mind.

"You said it yourself, this is your only lead. If we can get you dressed up nicely so you don't look out of place, I'm sure you'll be able to find something."

I had to think about this for a minute. I wasn't used to working with a partner, and I needed to be free from distractions—and very few women were as distracting as her. On the other hand, I was racing against the clock; if I didn't figure it out by Friday I'd have to give up, so I couldn't really afford to have wasted a whole day. And really, I had no reason to expect any kind of violent threat, as long as we were up here.

"Alright, you can come with me. For now."

"Thank you," she replied, jumping up to grab my hand. "So, where do you want to go first?"

"I have the names of a few people who were discussing Ascended Employment online. If you know anything about them, that would give us a good place to start." I retrieved my phone and opened up the messages. She read over the list, commenting as she did so.

"I do recognize a few of these. Nick Irwin, Bernard Horton, Amy Fuller... Yeah." Fiona nodded with recognition. "They all run together; some people call them the Cocktail Crew. I'd say they're pretty well known as spoiled brats, even up here. I can absolutely believe this conversation happened."

"So you've heard of them, then? Is there any way you might be able to introduce me to one of them?" I asked. She furrowed her brow, and an expression of discomfort appeared as she stared at the postings. "Sorry, I don't want to put you in an unpleasant situation. I can always try something else."

"It's… it's alright. It's just that a message out of the blue might seem suspicious, that's all. Unless…" Fiona walked off to the kitchen. I hesitated, but eventually followed her in. She shuffled through a drawer before pulling out a small, intricate card. She handed it over, and I studied it. The thick, layered paper extended an invitation to a ball, scheduled for tonight. "Here. Knowing them, I'm sure they'll be there. I had no intention of going, but if it will help, it's not too late to RSVP."

A party on a Tuesday seemed odd, but when there's no work in the morning, I suppose it doesn't much matter what day it is.

"Alright, that seems like a good plan, but we've got four hours until then."

"That's not a problem," she replied, stepping close for a moment. "You're going to need that long to get ready."

She slipped past and out of the room, leaving me alone and perplexed.

"Get ready?"

"Well you can't go to a ball dressed like that, can you?" I looked down at my clothes, worn and beginning to show their age. They certainly weren't fashionable, but I liked them.

"I don't think I own anything fancy enough for a ball," I said. Her full, red lips shifted into a bemused smile.

"Something told me you didn't, but don't worry about that. I'll take care of everything." She disappeared around the corner and through another threshold. What had I just gotten myself into?

## <u>Tuesday Evening</u>

"Perfect. Now, what's your name again?" Fiona asked, tweaking the red bow tie around my neck. I stood before the mirror in a tuxedo that had probably cost more than everything in my flat combined. It was close to the right size, but clearly tailored for someone else. My hair, typically a bit untidy from wearing a hat, was now smoothed and gelled into a professional, fashionable style like the people at the aerocar terminal.

"Raymond Navarro. I'm a biotech entrepreneur from Los Angeles and we met six months ago at your father's sixtieth birthday party," I answered, reciting the cover story she'd come up with casting me as her rich new boyfriend from out of town. It had worked on Magmell Security when they called inquiring about her guest, so it'd definitely be good enough for the ball. As long as I could keep up the act, that is.

"Excellent. As long as we stick together, there shouldn't be a problem," she said. "Now, it's my turn to get ready. Have a seat, I'll be as quick as I can."

I sat down on a nearby sofa, and the fabric of the suit glided across the soft upholstery. I prepared myself for the affair ahead. If someone had told me three days ago that I'd be spending time in Magmell, rubbing elbows with the rich and famous, I'd have laughed in their face. I had no experience with a formal event like this, and no reason to think I'd ever get it. With the anxiety mounting, I tried to take my mind off it by going over the case.

After a while, the whoosh of a door grabbed my attention, and I turned around just as it slid open. She was positively stunning; a sleek and sexy crimson red dress, fitted but still modest. The sequins lining her waist glittered and shone each time she drew breath. A dark pendant rested lightly on her chest, just inches above a hint of cleavage.

"You seem a bit distracted," she said, a coquettish smirk on her face. "Are you ready to go?"

"Uh… yeah. Right. Let's go." Fiona walked past, a slinky, flaunting walk that would send a monk fleeing to his confessional. It was all I could do to follow her out the door without staring.

The aerocar waited outside, with the driver leaning up against it. He looked up from his phone and greeted her with a tip of the hat, to which she returned a nod.

"Isn't this a little unnecessary?" I asked. "I mean, I'm not particularly familiar with the area, but we could probably walk there, couldn't we?"

"Ah, Lance, it's all about appearances. A wealthy entrepreneur would not walk to the party, and if he did, he wouldn't win much respect," she explained, seated across from me in the inward-facing seats of the aerocar. She crossed her legs as best she could. "Besides, it's on the next level up. Now just relax and let me handle this."

Shortly thereafter, we arrived in front of the massive hall, a building styled to look like an old-fashioned southern plantation. It was completely unlike any other building in the upper levels, with its white wooden siding and massive Roman columns. Resting at the top of the pillars was a triangular facade that covered the entrance. Four rows of large, evenly spaced windows spread out along both wings of the building, giving it a looming presence over its surroundings. I was brought back from my amazement by a hand softly coming to rest on my knee. I turned back around and looked at Fiona, who gestured for me to exit the vehicle. I hopped down to the ground and helped her out.

"Just follow my lead," she said as she walked past. Her steps transformed into a confident strut before my eyes, and her high heels left her hips swinging more consistently than a clockwork pendulum. Maybe Fiona doesn't like this world, but she definitely knows how to exploit it.

I quickened my pace to catch up with her, trying to keep my mind on the task at hand. This wasn't a date, after all—it was an investigation. As we approached, a man dressed as an antebellum-style butler turned to us.

"May I have your name, madam?"

"Fiona MacLeod. This is my guest, Raymond Navarro," she replied, with a kind of practiced condescension which I'd never heard from her before. The butler flipped through a distinctly anachronistic tablet list before looking up.

"Ah, Miss MacLeod, here you are. Welcome." The butler's eyes shifted over to me, and I struggled to feign disinterest. "And welcome to you as well, Mister Navarro. Please enjoy yourselves. The ballroom is the second door on the left."

Fiona headed inside without acknowledgment, and I followed close behind, eyes focused straight ahead.

The ballroom was a huge space, and the crowd justified its size; hundreds of guests were already dancing and mingling. A small band made up of Magmell residents indulging their artistic side sat in the corner of the room playing classical music. The tune emanated from the high ceilings, through unseen speakers hidden away so as not to ruin the aesthetic. Looking around, all I could think about was how the net worth of the people in this room had to be greater than that of a small country. The party guests wore a variety of outfits, some more reserved than others. Many of them dressed for the period, wearing hoop skirts or double-breasted jackets. Others wore more modern fashions, gowns so bizarre they'd even look out of place on a Parisian runway. Fortunately, the tuxedo seemed a common enough choice for men that I wouldn't draw attention.

"Alright, I'm going to have to make the rounds and exchange pleasantries. Stick with me and make sure to keep your stories straight," Fiona said, then dove into the crowd with me in tow. She came up to a group of middle-aged couples already chatting with each other.

"Keep it under your hat, but I heard that Gyrospec is planning to open a new branch there. Things might pick up soon," one of the men said as we approached. His date caught sight of Fiona, and her face lit up.

"Oh, Fiona, dear! It's been so long since I've seen you at one of these. How have you been?" she asked as they engaged in a quick embrace.

"Hey Tricia! I'm doing fine, thank you. How are you and Blake doing?" Fiona pulled back and nodded towards the other couple. "Todd, Nadine." They nodded back, Todd lifting his glass briefly in acknowledgment.

"We'd be doing a whole lot better if the situation in northern Africa would settle down," the man replied. "It's been wreaking havoc on the market lately."

"It's terrible, isn't it? Right when things had begun to settle down, the insurgency appeared," Fiona agreed. "They can't seem to catch a break."

"The Sudanese government is just lucky they have the Arin Group on their side," Todd said. He sipped lightly from the fluted glass before continuing. "If you're right about Gyrospec, Blake, then it may end soon."

I wasn't too up on world events, but what I had read didn't seem to agree with Todd's assessment of the situation. Blake glared at Todd briefly before restraining his irritation. His face shifted back into that faux-affable smirk that everyone seemed to have up here.

"Weren't the insurgents proven to be using equipment

provided by Gyrospec?" I asked. The smirk melted again. "I don't think the Arin Group is very likely to allow Gyrospec—"

"I'm sorry, but I don't believe we've been introduced," Blake interrupted, glaring at me with flat eyes and a brow furrowed in irritation.

"Oh my. I'm so sorry," Fiona said, turning back to me. She pulled me forward a few steps. "This is Ray, he's a west coast entrepreneur. He came out for an investor meeting, and I thought I'd give him the Magmell experience. Ray, this is Blake and Tricia. Blake was well acquainted with my father before he retired."

"A pleasure," he said, shaking my hand a little too firm. He struck me as a man who didn't like to be corrected. "Well, Ray, I'm not sure where you're getting your information, but I haven't heard any such thing. The Arin Group and Gyrospec only compete in the field of business."

That was a phrase that warranted a spit-take. It was the exact opposite of the truth, but a quick glance at Fiona told me I should let it go. The song that the band had been playing came to an end, and the loss of that background music made the growing pause all the more uncomfortable.

"Well, let's not forget that there are real people suffering there because of this," Fiona said.

"I've seen some positively ghastly stories coming from the more contested regions. It's just awful," Tricia agreed. "Why just last week my daughter Ashley—you remember her, don't you, darling?—well, she was telling me she wanted to volunteer over there in some kind of medical capacity. I nearly passed out from the shock! Her over there in that war zone… it's unthinkable! I do sympathize with her desire to help those poor people, but not if she has to risk becoming one of them."

"If you'd prefer she stayed somewhere closer to home, why not suggest she volunteer at the bottom of the Arcology?" I asked. The free clinic Mrs. Warner had spoken of came to mind. "There's no need to go halfway around the world if she's looking for someone to help. There are plenty of people right here in Kindred that could use her expertise."

All four of them stared at me now, expressions ranging from confusion to mild disgust. The reminder that thousands of people were suffering just a few floors below us wasn't a welcome one.

"Those... people at the bottom, they brought it upon themselves. They're lazy, filthy, violent little things. It's their mess, now they have to live in it," Tricia said at last. Before I could formulate a rebuttal, the music started back up, and Fiona took the opportunity to withdraw.

"Oh, is that Samantha over there?" she asked, looking off past Blake and Tricia. They turned to see. "That's the woman I was telling you about, Ray. Let me go introduce you. It was lovely seeing you again, Tricia, Blake. I hope you enjoy the rest of your evening."

She took my hand and led me away from the crowd to a calm area near the far wall.

"Lance, what are you doing?" she said, as quietly as she could manage over the music. "You can't talk about that sort of thing up here. People in Magmell absolutely do not want to hear about the bottom. It doesn't exist as far as most of them are concerned."

"I'm sorry, but I can't just listen to that kind of talk. Someone has to tell them the truth," I replied. If even I knew about Gyrospec, barely following the news, then there really was no excuse to be so misinformed.

"They don't want to hear it. Doing things like that are going to draw the wrong kind of attention. Remember, we're here to learn about Ascended. Isn't that what's important right now?" I looked to the floor sheepishly. She really was taking it seriously, and I needed to be on the same level.

"You're right, sorry." Fiona sighed and placed a hand on my shoulder. I looked up into her green eyes.

"I didn't mean to snap, but doing things like that will really hurt our chances. Just let me do the talking from now on, okay?"

"Okay."

As we headed back into the crowd, a woman in one of those strange gowns ran up to her, stopping far too close for comfort.

"Oh my God, Fiona? It's been forever!" she said, with the kind of enthusiasm that only emerges after a few drinks.

"Oh, hey Amy." Fiona's disgust slipped through as she awkwardly backed away to maintain some breathing room. She put up a peppy facade before continuing. "It has been too long, hasn't it? A year, at least."

"Yeah. That dress is from like, twenty-fifty at best, and you definitely had it when we were partying. Speaking of, how do you like mine?" Amy spun around a little too quickly and nearly lost her balance. "I got it straight from Riviera himself, you know. It's twenty thousand off the rack—or, it will be, when it's officially released. This one's special, prerelease. I keep trying to get him to make me something custom, but he always ends up mass producing it. So frustrating."

"It looks fabulous on you. Really, I can't imagine a better fit."

"So... what, uh... what have you been up to?" she asked, but didn't wait for an answer. "Oh! There was something I've been meaning to tell you, but you haven't been around in so long. Here, come with me."

She pulled Fiona toward her, off to a less crowded area near the wall. I tried to follow, but Amy stopped and stared at me.

"Who's this guy?" she pointed in my general direction.

"Oh, this is Ray. He's here with me, visiting from out west," Fiona replied. Amy let her arm fall melodramatically and looked me over.

"Right, yeah... Nick's not going to be happy when hears this." She turned to address me directly for the first time. "This is lady talk, so you better go make yourself busy networking or whatever. That's why people like you come to these, right?"

I glanced over at Fiona, who gave me a little shrug. She held up a finger, asking for a moment alone.

"You got me," I said. "Hoping to meet some investors for a startup I'm backing."

Amy nodded sagely, impressed with her own brilliance. "Well, you go do that. Bye bye."

I walked off a little ways down the wall, trying to keep out of the larger crowd. Fiona wouldn't leave me alone for long; I just had to keep to myself until she managed to break away from Amy. I decided to check out the refreshments table while I waited. Lunch with Fiona had been great, but skipping out on breakfast was starting to catch up with me. Besides, it was free food, and I needed to take advantage of that whenever I could.

As I waited, a man came up to the table and placed an order for a drink with one of the servants nearby. It was set up so that guests could help themselves, but the servant bowed his head and dutifully prepared a drink to the man's specifications. Upon closer inspection, I recognized him as Jake, from the photos online. He watched the servant pour each liquid with a flat expression. Talking to him might be a good way to do some digging, but he'd probably be gone before Fiona got back. I decided to stall him.

"Not exactly the most thrilling party ever, is it?" I asked. Based on the pictures I'd seen this was downright ordinary for them.

"It certainly isn't. I can't understand the fascination with these theme parties. Old traditions were left behind for a reason." Jake took his drink within seconds of its completion and swallowed half of it in one giant swig. He looked over at me with his eyes narrowed slightly, trying to figure out if he should recognize me. "I can't seem to recall—have we met before?"

"We wouldn't have, no." I extended my hand, and Jake shifted his drink from to his left and took it. His handshake was about as tough and sincere as a toddler's. "The name's Ray. I'm here visiting from out west. Just hoping to make some connections up in Magmell. Heard good things about this place."

"Oh, sure you are. Naturally. Let me guess, you've done your research? Hoping I might put in a good word to old Dad?" His voice was positively acidic.

"No, I just—"

"Yeah, right. Go fuck yourself, Ray." Jake chugged the rest of his drink and slammed the glass down on the table. He shot me a nasty look before marching off back into the crowd. I turned to the servant, who just stared back as if he'd seen nothing. I sighed and went back to the snacks. Maybe I could just shut up and keep myself out of trouble until Fiona returned as long as my mouth was full.

Of course, it could never be that simple. After about ten minutes, a man with long bangs that rebelled against copious amounts of hair gel stumbled over to the wall. It looked like he was trying to fight off a fit of dizziness.

"Hey, guy." He righted himself and turned to face me. "Hey. You... you're here with Fiona?"

"Yes." I answered hesitantly. "I am."

"Are you with her, though?" He crept a little closer, and I could smell the booze all over him. I had no doubt that he'd already been completely wasted before he walked into the building, and for an instant I wondered how he got through the front door like this. Then I remembered the power of a name.

"Excuse me?"

"Are you with her? Are you—are you..." I could tell what he was trying to say, even if he couldn't bring himself to spit it out.

"We're not that serious." I looked back, hoping to grab Fiona's attention, but no luck.

"Augh..." he let out a sound like a kicked puppy. "It's true. I thought Bernie was just fucking with me again. You think you're good enough for her?"

"What?" Just who the hell was this guy?

"Where is she?"

"I'm not—"

"FIONA!" the man shouted. I tried to step back to show that I wasn't associated with him, but people were already starting to gawk in horror. Amy and Fiona had heard him, and were pushing this way.

"I told you he wasn't gonna take it well," Amy said as they approached. Fiona's cheeks were glowing red with embarrassment.

"Oh, Fiona, you're really here... It's been so long. How—how you been?" he asked in a low voice. He straightened himself up, struggling to fake the appearance of sobriety.

"What are you even doing, Nick?" Fiona said, in the harshest whisper I'd ever heard. "You're embarrassing yourself, and now you're dragging me into it."

"I heard you're here with this guy." He grabbed the front of my coat, and I knocked his hand away. "Look at him, he's pathetic. His suit isn't even fitted right. You should come back to us. We've been—been having such a great time lately. Last Saturday we were out at RazMem in Vegas—"

"I'm not putting up with this again." Fiona grabbed my hand and marched outside.

We burst through the door outside and walked right past the butler. Fiona retrieved her phone and began summoning the aerocar back.

"Hey, Fiona..." I started, but I really had no idea what to say. After all, the reality of the situation was that I barely knew her. "Are you okay? I'm sorry you had to go through that because of me."

"No, I'm the one who should be apologizing," she said, looking down and running a hand across her face. "I thought I could get what we needed out of them quickly and disappear before something like that happened. You shouldn't have had to be involved with that."

I glanced out at the skies, looking for a sign of the aerocar's approach. The storm had passed a few hours ago, leaving the skies clear in its wake; a nearly full moon was still rising slowly over the cityscape. It seemed we had a moment to talk.

"So… I take it your relationship with the Cocktail Crew was a little more than just hearing about them."

"I guess I do owe you that much." Fiona sighed, and her gorgeous green eyes arose to meet mine. "I was friends with them. A shallow, party-based kind of friendship, but friends nonetheless. At the time, it was just fun. Now, though… I can't believe that I spent time with people like that. That I was like that."

She tucked the phone in her purse and faced away, staring at the ground once again. A stiff breeze rustled the grass before us, and the dull sounds of the party were carried over along with it.

"It's in the past. There's no point in feeling bad about things you can't change. Just do your best to move on, and keep trying to be a better person." I hesitantly put a hand on her shoulder. She reached up and placed hers atop mine. "And I think you've done a great job of that, from what I can see. I mean, you're helping me find this missing girl, and there's no real benefit for you in it. Heck, you even put yourself in an uncomfortable position to do so. That's pretty admirable, in my book."

Fiona glanced back, first at our hands and then at me. "Well… thank you, Lance. I hope you're right."

"Speaking of—why did you decide to help me?" I asked, withdrawing my arm as her hand dropped away. "Don't get me wrong, I'm glad to have your help, but I can't figure out why you'd be so willing to help a random detective who did some work for you once."

"Oh." She breathed deeply, as if debating whether to share the truth. "It's… complicated. There are a lot of reasons. Part of it was just seeing what it's like down on the surface. That day that I ended up at your office, I was coming back from Logan's apartment. I wanted to visit myself, to see if maybe he was just ignoring my messages. He would get all wrapped up in his work and forget to eat, even when he was living with me. Maybe he just forgot to check. So I went down there to where he'd said he lived, and I almost couldn't believe it. Walking through his building, just seeing how he lived... it was eye opening. I couldn't bring myself to actually look inside."

"He lived like that to protect you and the rest of your family." The aerocar's distinct muted blades echoed through the mild evening air, and it came around to land, but Fiona didn't move.

"No—I mean, yes, he did. I know that. But he was worried about those people long before he was living there. He always wanted to help them. And if Logan thought it was worth risking his life to help people, then maybe that's how I should honor him."  She touched the lapel of my tuxedo when she said his name, and I suddenly realized why she had a men's suit lying around. She gave a weak, insincere laugh. "Although, I must admit this isn't really what I had in mind. Probably should have just opened a charity or something."

A shout sounded out behind us, and we turned in time to see Nick getting dragged out of the party by his friends. Not wanting to take part in another scene, Fiona and I exchanged a glance and walked over to the aerocar.  I helped her up into the vehicle and we were soon underway.

We rode in silence for a moment, but as it occurred to me that our time together was ending for the night, I decided to speak up.

"So... what do you think we should do from here?" I asked. She ran a hand across her cheek, collecting her thoughts.

"I tried to get some information from Amy, but obviously I didn't get very far before things started going wrong. We can try again in the morning, when she's had a chance to sober up."

"Probably a good idea." I leaned back, looking out the window. Even up here, the city's lights were too bright to make out any stars, but it made for a surprisingly beautiful sight itself. From up so high, you'd never guess how much crime and corruption and filth flowed down those streets each day. No wonder the wealthy wanted to live here—everything looked so small and insignificant. Even the skyscrapers downtown looked like the roots clustered around the base of a cypress tree by comparison.

The aerocar descended onto the pad outside her apartment, and the door opened to let her out. She turned to me before getting up.

"I'm sorry if this has been a wasted day for you. I know we didn't make a lot of progress."

"Don't apologize for that, Fiona. I don't consider it a waste," I said, and she smiled. "Let me know in the morning if you manage to get in touch with Amy or one of the others."

"Alright." She started to get out of the vehicle, and once her feet hit the ground, she turned around and leaned back in. "You know, there was one more reason why I agreed to help you."

"Oh yeah? What is it?" I asked, sitting up.

"You decided to honor my brother's memory. The people he was fighting weren't able to get away with it because you got his work out to the world. You proved that you're an honest man, and that's rare these days." I was stunned, struggling to think of a response. She didn't wait for it. "Good night, Lance. I'll see you tomorrow."

"Oh… good night."

## <u>Wednesday</u>

I was sitting in my office, just starting to reread *Farewell, My Lovely* when Fiona called the next morning. I expected her to simply tell me when I could catch a ride to Magmell, but it seemed there was something else on her mind.

"Well, I have something I wanted to run by you before you come up here," she said. She sounded reluctant to even mention it.

"Oh?"

"I wasn't able to get up with Amy again... but Nick sent me a message this morning. An invitation to his place. He wants to apologize to both of us in person."

"You say that like it's a good thing." I got up and put the book back on the shelf. No time for reading this week.

"Nick was the one who suggested Ascended in the post. He might be our only real shot at getting to them."

"Are you really okay with that?" I asked. Her split-second of hesitation answered that for me.

"I'd have preferred going through Amy or Bernie, but it's hard to deny that Nick is the best bet. I should be able to deal with him when he's not drinking."

"You sure about this? I wouldn't want—"

"I'm sure. The sooner, the better, though."

"I'll leave right away," I said. I grabbed my hat and coat off the rack and set off for Arin terminal.

Fiona's driver was there waiting, and after one uneventful trip through the unusually sunny skies, I found myself in Magmell once again. Fiona came out to greet me, her crimson hair aglow in the summer sun.

"You weren't kidding about the coat," she said as we walked down the hall.

"Definitely not."

"Well, I'm afraid it isn't the most appropriate choice for a visit to Nick's if you want to maintain your cover." She lifted her hand, and the door to her apartment slid open. "Don't worry, I'll find you something."

Fiona disappeared into the back room, and returned a few minutes later with a modern looking, pastel green button-up shirt and khaki dress pants. I held them up to the light and sighed. Pastel was never high on my list, but if it was for the sake of passing, then so be it.

"Will we be taking the aerocar again?" I asked, returning in the new clothes. Fiona stood up from where she'd been waiting and fixed my collar.

"No, his place is close enough that we can walk without attracting negative attention."

"Is it really that bad to walk here? I mean, are the people here that lazy?"

"It's not about being lazy; it's a status symbol. You do it because you can afford to fly a million dollar vehicle half a mile down the road." She immediately walked off to find her purse. "Let's go."

Walking freely down the streets of Magmell, I had a chance to really look around for the first time. The area was a jumble of smoothly paved walkways, their serpentine paths winding between patches of private property. Pleasant little bushes lined the main route, with gardens of flowers in the grassy islands formed by their endless branching. I wondered for a moment who attended to these public spaces; it certainly wasn't the residents. Fiona stopped and headed off the path onto a brick sidewalk, which led to a fancy gate in a cast-iron fence. It was mostly for show, no doubt, but its presence emphasized the sheer size of the property. It spread out in a wedge shape, almost reaching the edge of the Arcology. A little more than half way back stood a huge, gaudy mansion. Its complex architectural styles went together like ice cream and sauerkraut; there were spires on the split-level roof, which was itself broken up by half a dozen dormers spaced irregularly across the front. A lone bay window, covered with a blackout curtain, faced the walkway. It was a house that catered to its owner's every whim, and the end result was something only its creator could love.

The double doors opened as we walked up to them, triggered by some kind of motion sensor. Nick, having heard the sound, emerged around a corner, his arms spread wide in welcome. As he noticed me, his brow furrowed.

"Thanks for agreeing to come over this morning, Fiona." He reached out and she allowed him a hug. He lingered just short of too long, then turned to shake my hand. The sleeve of his salmon-colored polo shirt slid back, revealing a fairly sizable bicep. "I was worried I wouldn't have the chance to apologize to you both personally. My behavior last night was just completely out of line, and I'm sorry you had to be a part of it."

"Let's just put it behind us, shall we?" Fiona placed a hand on my back and pushed slightly until I stepped forward. "I don't think you were properly introduced last night. This is Ray, he's an entrepreneur from L.A. He was in town on business and decided to stop by."

"I must apologize to you again for my unfortunate first impression. I hope you'll be able to look past it," Nick said, flashing one of the biggest, most insincere grins I'd ever seen as his attention fell on me. "Here, let's take this inside, shall we?"

He was far more polite and well spoken today, it seemed; a

lower blood-alcohol content can work wonders on manners. Fiona and I followed him into a parlor room, complete with a false fireplace, two chairs, and a couch, arranged to provide easy conversation. It almost looked classy, with its old oil paintings on the wall and a shelf of hardcover books, until I spotted the bright labels of cheap alcohol peaking through a half-open cabinet. Fiona sat down in one of the chairs, and Nick smoothly took a spot on the couch close to her.

"Nice place," I said, momentarily distracted as a butler entered the room. He was young, much younger than the ones at the ball last night.

"May I interest your guests in a drink, sir?" he asked, voice a little shaky. He turned to Fiona and I and began, "The bar is fully stocked—"

Nick shot him a glare so pointed I half expected it to draw blood. He fell silent, and it was only Fiona's quick response that salvaged the moment.

"I'll just have a glass of water, thank you," she said. I shook my head when he turned to me, and he scurried out of the room.

"So Fiona, it's been far too long. You never talk to any of your old friends any more," Nick said. "I do hope she's mentioned us to you. We all spent so much time together. Some more than others, of course."

"She's brought it up once or twice." This was definitely going to be a fun conversation. I smoothed out the legs of the slacks and reminded myself why we were here.

"You know how it is. I had so many things to deal with, and then Logan disappeared..." Fiona's voice trailed off. Nick put on a serious face and shook his head.

"What a waste. He always seemed like such a smart boy, and to disappear like that... I just wish I'd gotten the chance to know him better. We'd have been great friends."

"I didn't know that you had ever actually spoken to him," she replied. His eyes grew wide.

"Well, I mean, that's what I'm saying. There was that one time, he and I, uh—" Lucky for Nick, he was interrupted as the butler returned with Fiona's water. She thanked him as she took the glass, and he turned to Nick.

"Will there be anything else, sir?" the butler asked.

"No," he said, then glanced over at Fiona and added, "thank you. That will be all for now."

The butler looked mildly confused, but left the room as instructed.

"What a nice attendant you've found. So polite and quick to respond," Fiona said. "I really wish I could find someone so reliable."

"Ah, yeah. I picked up three new servants a while back, and they've all proven quite reliable so far. I tried using robotic servants a few years ago, but they're just too... error prone. A human butler will always be superior, if you ask me. And besides, that allows me to pay a real person instead of some rental service."

"You'll have to give me a name, because I've had so much trouble lately. Magmell Security does its job a little too well sometimes." Fiona took a sip of water and set the glass on an end table. She placed her hands in her lap very delicately, trying to put forward the most ladylike appearance possible. It struck me as the kind of thing she did more to maintain composure for her own sake than out of etiquette.

"They can be quite problematic at times, can't they?" Nick agreed. "I hope you didn't have any problems with them, uh— I'm sorry, but I'm just terrible with names. If it's not something that's important right away, it just slips out of my mind!"

"It's Ray," I said. I tugged at my shirt cuffs, trying to make the too-short sleeves a little less obvious. "I can understand forgetting names. I tend to zone out and start looking around when I get bored. This is some really remarkable architecture here, by the way."

"If you'd like, I can have one of the servants show you around. They ought to know the place well enough by now to do that," he said, staring me in the eye for a moment before his gaze returned to Fiona.

As he called for the butler, I glanced at Fiona to see if it was alright for her to be alone with him. She gave me a look that said, "this is our chance."

"Yeah, I think I'd like that." I rose to my feet, and followed the butler out of the room.

Once we passed out of sight, I reached for my phone and started recording.

"Sir, we can start here if you like, or perhaps the outside would be better," the butler said once we were out in the hallway.

"Whichever is easiest for you. And by the way, there's no need for that 'sir' business," I replied. He paused, and his eyes narrowed a bit. When nothing happened, he resumed our tour through the house.

"This is the dining room. The chandelier was imported from Italy, I believe, with handcrafted pure silver arms and fittings."

"It's nice," I said reflexively. "You seem to know the place pretty well. Have you been working for Nick long?"

"No, sir. I only started three months ago." He gave me that strange look again.

"You know, I notice you're quite young compared to most of the staff I see working up here."

"A little younger," he said. "If you'll follow me through into here—"

"I was just wondering if perhaps you were hired through Ascended Employment." He jumped a little at the name, and looked around to see if anyone was within earshot.

"No, I'm afraid I don't know what you're talking about. I was hired through the traditional system. It's difficult, but possible," he said, and continued on into the next room. He was a bad liar.

"That's interesting. Which agency did you sign up with?"

"Trenton Guild," he replied. "Let's continue the tour upstairs, shall we?"

I followed him up the stairs. There was only one group authorized to provide housekeeping services up here, and that wasn't it. He led me into a large room decorated with a musical theme. The light-colored walls bore paintings of stylized trombones and saxophones and violins. A top-of-the-line audio system dotted the walls and ceiling at various points for maximum coverage. In the corner of the room, just past the edge of the wide windows, sat the focal point: an incredibly beautiful grand piano. I approached it slowly, admiring the slick black curves. The lids to both the sound board and the keys were closed, covered in a thick layer of dust. The music stand had a built-in screen with a number of visible fingerprints on it.

"This is an amazing instrument. I can't even begin to guess what it cost. It's a damn shame no one's putting it to use." I reached out to touch it, but he winced as my hand drew close, so I stepped back instead. "I tend to be more into the horns myself. Jazz, ska, that sort of thing. But I can appreciate a nice piano when I see one."

"I guess Nick used to play. He comes and sits in here sometimes, but I've never heard any music."

"It looks like he's been out of practice for a lot longer than you've been around," I said. "I'm very impressed you got into the Trenton Guild at your age. I've been told they never accept anyone under thirty-five."

"Oh. Well... I was able to get in because an uncle worked there." He nodded, putting up an expression like he was trying to recall the memory. It looked more like he was trying very hard to convince himself that it was true.

"Alright, I think that's enough. We both know that's not true. If there even is a Trenton Guild, they wouldn't send you to Magmell. Why don't we be honest with each other for a minute and have a little chat? Man to man."

He stared me down hard. Brown eyes twitching, studying my face, looking for some telltale sign of a trap about to be sprung. "You... don't belong up here, do you?"

"If you're asking if I'm from Magmell," I said, leaning onto the chair next to him, "the answer is no. I'm from the surface."

"That makes sense." He nodded and let his body relax a bit, clearly relieved to have finally figured me out. He sat down carefully on the piano bench. "How do you know about Ascended?"

"I'm looking into them, but they seem to run a tight ship. It's been hard to learn much of anything."

"Doesn't surprise me to hear that."

"Why's that?"

"I shouldn't be talking about this," he said, fidgeting with the buttons on his cuff.

"What do you think might happen if you did?" I asked. He glanced up at me with a sigh.

"I don't really want to think about it. Kick me out, at the very least."

"Isn't that all the more reason to discuss it?" He shook his head a few times and finally rested it in his hands. I pulled the chair up and sat down across from him. "Mind telling me your name?"

"It's Jerrod. Jerrod Carver," he said. He pondered something for a moment, then scoffed. "First time I've said my name since I got here."

"That's terrible, Jerrod. Working as a servant doesn't make you any less of a person."

"You oughta tell that one to Nick. I bet he'd find it hilarious."

"Does Nick treat you badly?"

"Only when he's drunk. So yeah, most of the time." Jerrod leaned his elbows on his knees. "Throws his empty bottles at us and makes us clean it up. Pukes all over his antique rugs and gets mad if we haven't found it before he wakes up. That sort of thing. The only thing that makes it even a little bearable is that he goes on trips pretty often. We just have to keep out of sight of his little nanny cams when he's gone."

"He has cameras? Will you get in trouble if sees us talking?" I asked, looking around. I spotted one of them, nestled in the carvings on a cabinet. It was so small you'd never notice it unless you were looking for one.

"Nah, he only cuts 'em on when he's out of town. He likes to check the live feed from wherever he is and then call and threaten us if he sees we aren't working."

"I'm sorry you have to deal with him. You deserve better than that."

"Yeah, well, people don't always get what they deserve." Jerrod rubbed his deep-set eyes and yawned. "Besides, it's not like I have much of a choice anyway."

"You need the work that badly?"

"Of course. Why else would I put up with this? It was my only choice. I had to come up here." He looked down and fell back into the chair, throwing his arms out wide in exasperation. The dining table shook slightly as his arm came down to rest on it, sending a tremor through the bouquet of silk flowers adorning the center.

"From the bottom of the Arcology?"

"Yeah. I've lived there since I was real little. My mom and dad were some of the first to move in, actually." For a moment, there was a hint of pride in his voice, but it faded quickly. "You know, back before everything at the bottom went to shit."

"I've seen how rough it can be," I said. His head shot up and his eyes began puzzling again.

"You've been down there? Didn't happen to run into a Karen Carver, did you?"

I shook my head. "Can't say that I did, sorry. Is that someone important to you?"

"That's my mom. She still lives there with my brothers and

sister."

"So you're here to support them."

"Yeah. My dad worked maintenance on the west end, but he was killed in a gang fight about two years ago. Just walking home, minding his own business..." Jerrod glazed over for a moment, then he shook it away. "Anyway, since then, it's been up to me. Tried to find something down there, but it's useless. Arcology maintenance has become so automated, and there're no real businesses any more."

"How did you learn about Ascended, then? I mean, Nick obviously didn't go around the bottom floor with a 'help wanted' sign."

He snorted. "Can you imagine? He'd be mugged within five minutes, probably dead on the corner in ten. No better than he deserves." He had a sadistic little smirk on his face at the thought. I could hardly blame him. "No, my sister found their pamphlet one day, gave it to me. Said they could hook us up with jobs at the top of the Arcology, and for good pay, too. Looked legit, since it was printed on that real glossy paper, ya know? It was pretty much the only job I'd heard of, so I went to their meeting. They promised they'd send money and take care of our families if we'd work as butlers or landscapers or maids."

He paused and took a deep breath. He ran his hand across his face, past the bags under his eyes and the small scars that marked off all those years of struggle and malnourishment.

"Anyway, I passed the interview. A few days later, they had us come to this spot along one of the supports. The guy there had a welding torch—never saw one of those before. He cut open a hatch on the support and there was a set of stairs inside. Pretty cramped, but I guess it was left over from construction or for maintenance or something. We had to walk all the way to the top. Sometimes there would be a really narrow pass between walls to get to the next stairs. Felt like forever climbing up here. When we finally got out, it was a big, kinda warehouse-looking place. I think it must have been in the—the bulkhead? Is that what it's called? It was in the space between different blocks. They taught us a few basics over the course of a week or so, and then kinda just lined everyone up in rows. The rich people came in, picked out whoever they wanted. Nick grabbed me because I was at the end. He took two other guys then, too, and brought us here."

"Wow. That's quite a story." It would make excellent evidence, should I need to expose the company. I went over the details in my head. "It must have been a tough choice to leave your family. Have you been able to communicate with them at all?"

"I haven't, but a few of the more senior servants have heard from theirs. It's hard to get a message to the bottom, ya know? They were pretty short, just little 'thanks, it's so much better now' kinds of things. Even a little note like that makes them so happy, though. It's all worth it if we can give our families a better life, right?"

"I suppose it is," I said. I wondered if I would have been able to do the same thing, in his place.

He stood up and stretched a little bit. "We should get going. Nick might come looking and I wouldn't want him to find me sitting around."

"Yeah, I guess not," I replied, standing up alongside him. "If you want, I could take a message back down to your family."

He grabbed my arm and turned me to face him. "Are you serious? You'd do that?"

"Of course. It's the least I can do after all of this." A smile appeared on his face for the first time, and he eagerly gave me their address. I closed the recording and handed him the phone, which he used to record a short video for them. "Oh, but there is one last thing—a girl named Melanie Warner. I believe she's a recent recruit of Ascended. Have you ever met her?"

"Nope, I don't think so. Depends how recently you mean, but it's possible she's still in training."

"Just thought I'd ask." I put the phone back and reached a

hand out to him. "I'm glad I had the chance to talk with you, Jerrod. I hope things get better."

"Um, thanks." He shook my hand, then awkwardly scratched his short curly hair. It seemed I'd managed to surprise him one last time. "Here, back out this way."

Jerrod led me back the way we came. As we descended the stairs, I saw Fiona and Nick talking near the door. Her face lit up briefly, and Nick turned around to see us.

"Quite a long tour. Did you enjoy it?" he asked, his gaze shifting from me to Jerrod and back again.

"Definitely. You have a very beautiful home. I hope I can have one like it some day."

"You'll never find another house like this one," he said dismissively. There was no arguing with that.

"Well, Nick, It's been nice catching up with you. Ray's only going to be back east for a little while, so he can't afford to miss his meeting tonight," Fiona said. I nodded in agreement.

"Yes, it's very important. I apologize if this cut your visit short," I said.

"What exactly are you in town for again?" Nick asked, staring me down.

"Meeting with investors for a cybernetics start-up. I probably shouldn't go into too much detail. It's not my information to give away, after all."

"Yes, of course. Well, good luck with that." He turned away and faced Fiona once more. "Now, don't be a stranger, Fiona! We all miss having you around. Wouldn't it be nice to hang out with your old crew again?"

"Oh, yeah. I'll see if I can work it into my schedule," she replied. "Be sure to call me when you've worked out a meeting for me."

"I'll get on that right away," he said, signaling for Jerrod to get the door. As it swung open, Nick said quietly, "goodbye. Take care, Fiona."

"You too. Goodbye, Nick."

"It was a pleasure. Goodbye," I said, looking over at Jerrod. The door closed, and I could still hear the muffled voice of Nick on the other side. I hoped he wasn't yelling at Jerrod on my account. We walked quietly until we passed through the front gates.

"Were you able to learn anything from the butler?" Fiona asked. She relaxed her posture now that we were a safe distance away.

"Some." I relayed the facts of Jerrod's story to Fiona.

"I'm sure this will come as no surprise, but that's not how Nick tells it." We stopped walking for a moment, and she sat down on a nice looking stone bench just a few steps from the path. Fiona looked over at me as I sat down beside her. "According to him, Ascended is some sort of charitable organization that helps people on the bottom find work. A good portion of Magmell doesn't agree with the strict rules regarding servants; Nick says that they'd prefer to hire people from right here in the Arcology, instead of the professionally trained butlers that typically make it through the screening process. So Ascended has taken to filling that niche directly, in spite of the rules. He swears that they're well treated and well paid."

"Well, sorry Nick, but I'm more inclined to believe Jerrod," I said. "How much of Nick's story is true, though? It's got to have some basis in fact."

"I can't say yet. That's why I asked him to set up a meeting with them for me."

"Wait, what? You can't do that." She stared at her feet, shifting them about like she was working up the courage to say something. In the silence, I could just make out the gurgling sound of a fountain nearby.

"Ascended is being run by this guy named Jake Freely, who joined up with Nick and the others a little after I left. I think it's safe to say that if he's partying with them, it's no charity. But, if he thinks I'm one of their friends, then I just might be able to get the truth out of him."

"I mean, it's not impossible," I said. I recalled his hostility from the night before, and the charity story became even harder to justify. No one who'd ever met the man would buy it, but there was no way I'd be willing to let Fiona put herself in danger. All I could think of was the conflict at Viacorp a few months ago. Overton had threatened not only me, but everyone else I'd spoken to during that case—Fiona included. I'd been lucky to make it out of there alive, and even an indirect threat like that was more than I wanted Fiona to deal with. Magmell was a world of Overtons, of people who could be every bit as vindictive and dangerous, and had the resources to get away with it. "Maybe people like Jerrod really do need this, even if it's not quite right."

"Come on. Even on its face, it doesn't make sense. What kind of protections would these workers have from being exploited? Once they're up here, they have to submit to every order, every whim, no matter how absurd. Jerrod even said as much, right? He can't risk losing this one shot at employment. A real charitable organization would never put them in that position."

I sighed and looked around. A light breeze shifted the green leaves and the thick, freshly cut grass. The fountain put on its eternal show, firing spurts of clean, clear water into the air in a strictly choreographed dance. The long shadow of a statue reached out toward us, as if begging for someone to appreciate the beauty that had been so painstakingly created here. No one walked by.

"We can't forget Melanie. I don't know if this is right or wrong, but I do know that my first duty has to be to my client. If getting her daughter back means leaving everything else, that's just how it's going to have to be."

"I can tell you're worried about me, but don't be. Nick

wouldn't take me somewhere dangerous," she said. I glanced back at Fiona, and our eyes briefly made contact. I had no doubt that she believed it.

"Alright. I'm going to wait until you've heard back from him to make a real judgment, but for now... okay."

"I understand that, I guess," Fiona said, with a little smile that I couldn't quite figure out. She rose to her feet and we resumed our walk.

On the way back to Fiona's apartment, we ran into a woman that I didn't recognize from the posting. She looked a little older than Fiona and wore a professional-looking business suit. Her dark hair was kept in a short bob style that was well-suited to her face. When she noticed us, she made her way over immediately. Fiona broke off to meet her halfway.

"Hey, Fiona! You busy?" she said as they hugged briefly. "Want to come up and have some lunch?"

"Sorry, Vivian, but I'll have to take a rain-check. I'm a little busy right now."

"Right, you've got a guest." Vivian nodded as I walked up beside Fiona. "I just thought you might want someone to talk to after last night. So sorry you had to deal with that. Nick's been a real mess lately."

"Tell me about it." Fiona sighed, and Vivian reached over, placing a hand on her shoulder.

"Don't blame yourself. When you cut him out, he could have taken it as a wake-up call, but he didn't. He chose to retreat into the bottle. That's on him." Vivian looked at her with a concerned expression until she made eye contact. They communicated wordlessly in that moment, and Vivian glanced over at me. "It seems like you're better off now anyway. Hang in there, and if you need me I'm just downstairs. I'm sure Karen would love it if you stopped by, too."

"Thanks," Fiona said with a little laugh. "I'll keep that in mind."

"Anyway, I'll leave you to it. I've got a long day ahead still, but I wanted to check in." I watched as she walked past, then turned back one last time. "Nice to meet you, too. Maybe next time we can actually talk to each other."

Vivian continued on her way, and Fiona gestured towards the elevator. I waited until the doors closed to speak up.

"Sorry, I don't mean to keep you from your social life. Don't let me stop you from going to lunch."

"You're not keeping me from anything, Lance. If you weren't here, I still wouldn't be going out," she replied, still facing forward.

"Don't like her?"

"That's not it. Vivian and Karen are great. I just..." she trailed off as the elevator came to a stop and the doors slid open.

"It's okay. You don't have to explain yourself to me. I just really don't want to cause you problems," I said. Fiona stepped out and turned around. She looked at me with a tender smile before setting off down the hall.

# Wednesday Evening

We spent a few hours at her apartment, beginning with a very lovely lunch. I had some time to kill, so I decided to look into Jake as much as I could before Fiona's appointment came around. He'd made very few social media posts; it seemed like he only kept up the profiles for appearances. Whatever had caused him to not list his family seemed to be mutual, as his father's page was similarly lacking in any mention of Jake. In the photos that Amy and the others had posted, he always had a big smile on and looked like he was legitimately enjoying himself. He also had a bottle in his hand in every one, often times something far stronger than what the others were drinking. A comment from Bernard implying they'd recently used Keralisk led me to believe that alcohol was probably among the least of his vices.

He was a student at Magmell University, at least according to his profile. None of his fellow students had much to say about him, however, and I wasn't even able to find out what classes he was taking. I wondered how he could afford living up here and attending a school as expensive as this one while on poor terms with his father. This, too, proved difficult to answer, but at the very least I was able to make a guess—his mother. Her page had several messages declaring her support for him, although Jake had done his best to keep it out of sight. Reading them over, they struck me as more self-serving than genuine. Still, there had to be some truth at the heart of it, and that would be enough.

I set my phone aside and took a break. The screen in the corner of the room spouted a stream of propagandist news as background noise, broken up with vapid banter between hosts. I wished desperately that I'd kept my book from this morning on me. I could have finished it by now.

At last, a muffled ring broke through the monotonous droning of the hosts, and I silenced the news as Fiona grabbed her phone. She closed her eyes for just a second, then answered.

"Hey, Nick," she said. "Thanks for getting back to me so quickly."

Fiona paced around in small circles, listening to his explanation.

"Today? Oh, I see… no, that makes sense," Fiona replied. "You don't have to do that. I can handle it on my own—" whatever he was saying, she crinkled her nose in disgust. "Alright, if you say so. See you then."

She hung up and set the phone back on the table.

"He was able to set up a meeting. For tonight, actually," she explained, walking over to join me. "But if I want to see them, Nick will have to go with me."

"Tonight? That's tough to reconcile with the cover we gave him earlier."

"I'm pretty sure the fact that you 'had plans' tonight is exactly why he set it up for then."

"I can't just let you do this alone. It's not your responsibility."

"Look, Lance, you know this is the most likely way to find Melanie. And we need to find out how they operate, right? There's not going to be a better chance than this."

I shook my head. "This was a mistake. You're too involved."

"Lance, I can make my own decisions." She stood over me, a determined expression on her face.

"Okay, fine. But you've got to understand, I can't just sit here while you're out doing all the work."

"They won't let me in if you come along."

"No, but I can follow behind, keep an eye on things." I got up and stood next to her. The late afternoon sun poured in through the windows. "Maybe I can even do a bit of reconnaissance from outside their compound."

"Alright, then. I'm supposed to meet Nick at seven, at a park on the other side of the Arcology."

"Okay. Make sure to keep your phone on you," I said. "If worst comes to worst, I can probably get someone to triangulate your position with it and find you that way."

"It's far, but I can walk, if that makes it easier to follow," she said, then started heading out of the room. She turned back as she got to the threshold. "Go ahead and take that shirt off. I'll see if I can find a less conspicuous one."

"What?"

"Well if you're wearing the same clothes, he's far more likely to spot you, don't you think?" Fiona walked into the guest bedroom and disappeared.

"Oh, right." I undid the buttons and was left standing there in an uncomfortable white undershirt. She returned carrying a dark blue button-up, and we traded. As I slipped my right arm in the sleeve, she stopped me.

"What happened to your arm?" Fiona took my left arm and studied the scars that covered the back of my hand. "When did this happen? It can't have been too long ago…"

"It's nothing, don't worry about it." I pulled away and finished putting the shirt on. "Are you ready? We don't have a whole lot of time."

"I'll… just be a minute." She walked back into her room, and I sat down to wait.

It wasn't long before we were walking at a brisk pace down the winding paths of Magmell. I kept my distance from Fiona, instead taking in the sights all across this level. The architectural diversity was impressive, for lack of another term; a few areas had unified styles, but there was a new look around every corner, and Nick was far from the only one with bizarre taste.

I came to a halt as we approached the park, within sight of the level's eastern edge. It was a pleasant, serene sort of space, with more large trees than I'd seen on Fiona's side. The shadows of tall apartment complexes behind me loomed forward, bringing the night with them. Fancy, old-fashioned streetlights kicked on along the paths, lighting up a cafe on the park's outer rim. Fiona walked up to a small rotunda on a raised platform, near the center of the park. She waited patiently, staring out at the clouds moving in across the horizon. A pair of men seated at the cafe stood up when they noticed her and made a beeline right to her. Fiona turned as they approached and greeted them. Nick went in for a hug, while the other man, presumably Jake, simply extended his arm and shook hands. They conversed for a few minutes before Jake gestured towards the outer loop, which ran around the entire circumference of this level.

I followed as they walked the loop, careful to keep back. They chatted quietly, with far more restrained body language than I'd come to expect from the residents of Magmell. Jake appeared to be quite subdued in general, as if he'd become used to keeping a low profile. Their journey wasn't long; Jake pointed to a house that was facing outward, nestled between two large apartment complexes with a few shrubs around it. It was much smaller than the apartments, and quite narrow. They turned off the path and disappeared inside.

Standing outside the apartments, I remembered what Jerrod had told me of his trip up here—traveling through the support pillars, stuck in the bulkhead... if this was their headquarters, there had to be access to the bulkhead. I studied the house until I spotted a small window along the foundation, indicative of a basement. Once I was sure the coast was clear, I slipped between the house and the apartment building, an alleyway about twice as wide as my shoulders. I knelt down behind the privacy hedges, careful not to make noise, and peered into the window.

It was dark, and for a second I thought the window was blacked out. Then the room lit up, and I could see a shadow coming down the stairs. It belonged to a small, weaselly man with a scowl chiseled into his face. His thin black hair was combed over his bald spot in a futile attempt at maintaining the illusion of virility. The man rolled up a solid gray rug, revealing the metal of the bulkhead underneath. He picked up a screwdriver and removed the screws in the corner of each plate, then lifted each one up and slid it off to the side. They were far thinner than they should have been; likely a cheap replacement for ease of access. Once all four were out of the way, the man pointed a flashlight down into the opening. With his other hand, he gestured for someone to come up, and a few minutes later, eight young ladies in French maid outfits emerged from the hole, forming up into two rows of four. The man cut off the flashlight and waggled it at them as he gave some instructions. Once it seemed like they understood, he smacked one of them on the butt with the flashlight, then laughed his way back up the stairs, leaving the girls alone.

There wouldn't be a better chance to talk to them than this. I knocked on the glass a few times, but none of the girls turned to investigate. A blonde girl twitched her head, curious but afraid to break formation. I tried knocking rhythmically, to the beat of the old "shave and a haircut" call and response, which seemed to do the trick. She turned around, confusion and worry printed across her face. I waved her over, and she seemed very hesitant. I pointed up, towards the house, and then shook my head, hoping to get across that I wasn't with these people. She grit her teeth and looked around the room again, hands anxiously grasping the front of her outfit. When it was clear I wasn't going anywhere, she finally broke from the line, drawing the attention of the other girls beside her. They tried to get her to return, but she pointed to the window and unlatched it, tilting it inward a few inches.

"Who are you? Are you trying to get us in trouble?" she asked in a hushed tone. "This is a test, isn't it?"

"I'm not sure how much time we have, so I'll cut to the chase. I'm looking for a girl named Melanie Warner, and I have reason to believe she's been recruited by Ascended Employment within the last two weeks. Do you know her?"

"No, I don't know anyone named Melanie. Now, get out of here before you get us fired," she replied hastily. One of the other girls who had been watching, a brunette, now came over to join her.

"D'you say Melanie? I think I know her," the new girl said. "She's in one of the other training groups, but she's in the same shelter as us."

I breathed a sigh of relief. At last, I had some solid confirmation that she was actually up here.

"Other training groups? Do you know where they are?"

"Sorry, can't say. She'll be in the shelter after nine, though. It's like... a ten minute walk from here, back that way." She pointed in, towards the center of the Arcology. "We're in shelter four. One thing, though: why are you doing this?"

I wanted to explain how the system up here would be used against them, to rob them of what little power they had left. How badly they might be treated. But I couldn't risk an outburst; if she got upset and lashed out at Jake and his crew, there was no telling what might happen to her. And regardless of how it turned out for these girls, it would definitely be bad for me.

"Melanie's mother didn't know that she left and got worried," I replied, as simply as possible. "Why? Is there something worse going on?"

The girl grew nervous, and the blonde from before had a 'don't you dare' look on her face.

"I don't know if it's true, but based on the way some of the guys training us have been acting, I wouldn't be surprised if it is. I heard a rumor when we got here that they might try pushing us into—" she began, but the sound of the door at the top of the stairs cut her off. The blonde girl scrambled back into line, and the brunette locked the window and fell in not long after. I backed away from the window as much as I could, just barely catching sight of Jake coming down the stairs as I left.

I walked out of the alleyway and went to sit in front of the apartment building next door, silently cursing their poor timing. There was still something more to this, but what could she have been trying to say? I considered some possibilities, all far too grim to think about for long, before heading back to wait in the cafe. I picked up a coffee from the ordering machine—outrageously expensive, up here—and sat down at a table outside. Time dragged on, until finally Nick and Fiona emerge from around the corner, walking calmly through the park. I got up and slipped out of sight.

They meandered through the paths, with Fiona keeping ahead at a quick pace, not looking back. Nick followed behind, saying something; his body language was strange, almost apologetic. As they reached the edge of the park area, Fiona said goodbye, and he reluctantly headed off. Fiona walked just far enough in the other direction that he wouldn't be able to see her and leaned back against a tree.

"Learn anything?" I asked as I walked up. She gave a heavy sigh in response.

"Well, Nick and Jake have an... interesting relationship. Very hot and cold. They're planning on having some drinks tomorrow night," she said, standing upright. We started back to her apartment.

"About Ascended, I mean."

"Jake told me about them, or at least, he gave me the same type of answer that Nick did. He insisted that they're just a group of concerned Magmell residents trying to help the people at the bottom." Fiona stared at the ground as we walked, watching the pebbles paved into the sidewalk pass by.

"They're consistent, at least," I replied. "Maybe it really is the truth? It's inevitable that some people will mistreat their servants, but if most of them are treated decently, and it helps their families back home, is it really wrong?"

"I don't know; if it really is so well-meaning, then this just strikes me as the wrong way to go about it. There's too much potential for abuse."

"True." The sun had passed below the city's skyline now, and the clouds that had once been on the horizon were gathering behind us. Stray leaves from the park rolled across our path in the evening breeze. "Anything else?"

"He explained the hiring process. There's a pretty steep 'administrative fee' initially, then regular payments that are sent to the families below, as dictated by their employers. He also showed off some of the new maids that will be up for hire. I didn't get a chance to talk to them in private, so I can't say whether Melanie was among them. Sorry."

"I saw them, too. Even spoke to a few of them briefly. One of them confirmed that Melanie is up here, and that I could find her in a place called 'the shelter' after nine, but that's right about when they brought you down. Did they happen to tell you when these maids would be available?"

"They're having another... expo, or whatever you want to call it, Friday morning. According to Jake, they contract about eighty percent of the group at each one, so odds are that Melanie will be picked up by someone there," Fiona said. I sighed, looking up at the streetlights lining the way back. They flashed on all at once, twin trails of soft and brilliant lights spiraling across Magmell.

"Well, that certainly complicates things. Tomorrow night will be our only shot at getting in touch with her before she's hired out." I had no idea exactly how we'd manage to pull that off, however. The shelter had to be in the bulkhead, but those areas are for systems and maintenance only. Finding a place to enter it from up here would be difficult, and that was assuming that Ascended hadn't found a way to block them all off, just in case.

"You aren't going to stop the whole operation?" Fiona asked, coming to a halt. I turned back to face her.

"I told you, I don't think we're capable of that. And at this point, I'm not even sure that it's the right thing to do."

Fiona glanced down at her feet, as if she had something to say, but wasn't sure how. Her head rose slowly until she made eye contact.

"Those girls, the maids… they looked scared. I could see it in their eyes, in their faces. I certainly don't know anything about living in poverty, but I'm positive that what they're afraid of isn't a lost job opportunity."

I thought back on the girl from the basement, her half-finished sentence echoing through my mind. "One of them did try to tell me about some rumor she'd heard, but she never got the chance. Whatever it was, the other girl didn't want her to mention it."

"I bet it had to do with those outfits they had on. Didn't you think they were strange? They're not exactly the norm up here."

"Do you think it's supposed to be demeaning? Objectifying?" It seemed obvious as soon as I said it; of course it was. The possibility of sexual exploitation hadn't even occurred to me. I shuddered, as if my body was physically rejecting the thought. The subtle pressure of fingernails digging into my palms made me aware of just how tightly I'd been clenching my fists since she finished.

"So? Does that change anything?" Fiona asked, staring up at me sternly. I remained silent. This had to be what that girl was trying to tell me.

"Well… yeah," I said at last. "I just don't think there's any way the two of us can do anything about it on our own before Friday."

This revelation might have influenced my feelings on getting involved, but it wasn't going to change the reality of the situation. I couldn't just bust in the doors, guns blazing. Especially not after Viacorp.

"There has to be something." Standing there in the growing darkness, I had no idea what it could be. I shook my head and started walking again.

"Let's get back to your place for now. We can discuss it more there."

Our trek through the Magmell twilight concluded without another word. We entered her apartment, and Fiona dropped herself onto the nearest sofa in an exaggerated fashion. She leaned back, resting her head on the cushions and staring up at the ceiling. I walked around and sat down across from her.

"Perhaps we should call it a night; figure out a plan tomorrow. After all, there's no way we can do something tonight," I said, sitting forward to rest my elbows on my knees.

"I suppose. I definitely need to relax some after today," she sighed, then sat upright.

"I can understand that. I might grab a drink and unwind a little myself when I get back. Sometimes that's just what you have to do with a tough case."

"Well, you don't have to go home to get a drink. After dealing with Nick all day I could use one myself." she perked up slightly, and rose to her feet. "What do you like?"

"Scotch is my drink. I can't afford to indulge too often, but it's always a treat when I do."

"I guess I shouldn't be surprised," Fiona said, ducking into the kitchen. After a moment, she peeked her head around the corner. "I'm afraid I don't have anything too hard. Haven't been keeping it on hand lately. I do have plenty of wine, if that interests you."

"Eh, why not? As long as it's nothing too expensive. I'd hate to be drinking some rare vintage without even knowing it." I didn't have much experience with fine wines. Or cheap ones, for that matter.

Fiona disappeared behind the corner again, setting off a cascade of sound from cabinets and drawers, culminating with the pleasant ring of two empty glasses clinking together. She returned with a bottle, a bottle opener, and a pair of wine glasses, which she set on the coffee table between us.

"So, is there anything else you do to relax?" she asked, as the bottle opener drilled into the spongy wood.

"I like to read, occasionally watch an old movie if I can get my computer to cooperate. I'm not the most exciting man in the world, sorry to say," I replied. The cork made a dull pop, and she set it aside.

"I wouldn't say that. You're an unusual guy." Fiona poured the wine; first into my glass, then hers. I picked it up and tilted it toward her in thanks. "I bet you read a lot of old detective stories, don't you?"

"What makes you say that?"

"Oh, come on, Lance. Look at yourself for a moment. I remember the first time I came into your office. You had your feet kicked up on the desk, half-open venetian blinds behind you. You wore a fedora and trench coat up here in the middle of summer. You can't tell me that's all just a coincidence."

"It's a very practical outfit." I grinned sheepishly from behind my glass. The wine was incredibly dry—or at least, I think that's how you'd describe it.

"I'm sure," she teased. "It's a little odd to me, but I like that about you."

"The outfit?"

"No, not the outfit. The whole detective act. You're living your dream, and I can't help but admire that," Fiona said. She brought the glass up to her vibrant red lips and took a sip. "Although, the cynical part of it doesn't really suit you."

"And what makes you say that?"

"You're a hopeless romantic. You idealize the image of a profession from a hundred years ago." She slid forward a little, and leaned in. "In fact, I might even go so far as to say that you're pretty much a modern day Don Quixote."

"Lucky for me that the nearest windmills are a few hundred miles away, then," I said, taking another drink. Fiona laughed, and a wonderful little smile appeared on her face. It was impossible not to smile back. "I don't think I'm that much a romantic. There's a little more to it than that."

"Well, okay. Take this case with Melanie, for example." She set down her glass and started filling it again. "She's from the bottom of the Arcology, right?"

"Yeah, she is."

"So there's no way her mother is going to be able to pay you for all this." She held the bottle toward me, so I finished my glass off and let her refill it.

"A pro bono case is good every once in a while," I replied. Fiona just shook her head and laughed again. "Where is my coat, anyway?"

"You and your coat. Where did you even find it? It looks like real leather."

"It—it was my grandfather's. He left it to me when he passed," I said. "The hat, too. And the books."

"Oh..." She was quiet for a moment, the respectful sort of quietness that travels alongside the mention of death. "You must have had a pretty great relationship with him."

"My dad... he was in the Drone War when I was a kid. He didn't come back." I looked down at the half-full glass, wondering just how much of this honesty I could actually chalk up to it. Not as much as I'd like. "My mom spent all her time working to make up the difference, so I ended up with my grandparents a lot. He'd tell me all these stories, about being a detective back in the eighties... they were ridiculous. Exactly what a kid wants to hear."

Fiona placed a hand on my knee, but I wasn't really in the mood for wallowing in memory. I crossed my legs, and she withdrew.

"Okay, I think that's enough about me. What about you? You said that this place used to belong to your grandparents, right? How'd you end up here?"

She brushed her crimson locks out of her eyes and sighed. "Well, my grandfather was a big supporter of the Arcology, back when it was first proposed. Not on the board or anything, but people like him were instrumental in getting it built. Both he and my grandmother were very hopeful about it. They reserved a space right at the top before construction even began." Fiona paused and set her glass down. "She never did get to live up here."

"I'm sorry to hear that."

"Don't be. I'm always hesitant to say this around the family, but... I'm kind of glad that neither of them lived long enough to see how it is today. The way that the bottom ended up would break his heart." I took the last sip of my wine, and she lifted the bottle to fill it again. "He died about ten years ago, right after Magmell University opened. I was accepted to the first class, so I started living here that summer. Logan joined me here five years back, when he was accepted."

"You've lived up here a long time, then," I said. I resumed drinking, its effects just beginning to make their presence known.

"Yeah. Nearly my whole adult life, in fact. The culture up here, it gets to you... in ways you could never predict. Logan couldn't tolerate it, and it was only after he left that I started to notice," she said. Her emerald green eyes were staring so far off I thought she might be trying to see into the afterlife itself. Fiona filled her glass again and tossed it back. "Next month, it'll have been two years since he moved out, you know. It doesn't feel like it's been that long. Sometimes I still expect him to be sitting here when I come home."

The room fell silent, and I drank a little more. Maybe this had been a mistake, digging up old memories. I didn't want to depress her, after all. "That's right around the time you stopped hanging around with Nick and the others, isn't it?"

"'The cocktail crew.' It's a dumb name, don't you think? We didn't even drink cocktails very often. Too much trouble," she said, watching as little bubbles streamed up the sides of her glass. "We drank everything else."

"What made you decide to leave? Was it just Logan?"

"No… it wasn't just that." Fiona let out another sigh and melted back into the overstuffed cushions. "We didn't really spend time together as a group when sober. It was always drinking and partying, wild crazy things that, in hindsight, were pretty cruel. But back then, it was just fun. It's what everyone was doing, what kept us together in the evenings. What drove everyone away from each other in the mornings, as quick as possible. There was always a lot of drama, but it would blow over as soon as the next party came up. And it was like that for years.

"Then, maybe two, two and a half years ago, Nick and I started getting a little closer. When Logan left, and I cut back some, he started to call me up so we could spend time together. Without the others. Without drinking… and he still wanted to do those kinds of things. Wanted to harass the waiters at the expensive restaurants, wanted to bribe the chauffeurs to let him take aerocars out on joyrides. For the first time, I could really see how awful that kind of behavior actually was. It's not all in good fun, it's not just drunken antics. It was dangerous, and despicable, and most of all, immature. And it was as clear as day, then, what I had to do."

"So that was the end, huh?" I said.

"That was the end."

The conversation lulled for a moment, and I finished off my glass. Fiona picked up the bottle to refill it, but I waved it away. "No thanks, that's enough for me." I set it down and then continued. "I know you don't like them now, but did you at least have fun with them at the time?"

"I did. Even at the end, when it was just Nick and I, it wasn't always bad. We'd go back to his place and he'd play piano for me. He tried to teach me how to play, too, but I didn't quite have the dexterity for it. I'm much better at the violin." She smiled as happier memories came to the surface. "The first few years at university were the best, though. I remember one night, we snuck some wine bottles out, and Bernie wanted to—"

Fiona stopped mid-sentence, and her eyes grew wide. She looked over at me, giddy with realization. "That's it!"

"What? What's it?"

"I know how to get between floors."

She leapt to her feet, and held the bottle up. I winced, anticipating a spill. "It can be kind of hard to get alcohol underage here, but there was always a ton of demand for it. Whenever we'd get some, we would go to this broken maintenance hatch nearby and drink in the tunnel. There was so much broken glass there... I know they tried to fix it a couple of times, but the teenagers always found a way back in. I bet it's still there now."

"That's fantastic!" I jumped up as well, then paused. "What if Ascended has already blocked it off?"

"Well, that's the thing. The tunnel didn't go very far. There's a gate maybe thirty feet from the hatch. You'd need a keycard to gain entrance past that point."

"I might be able to work around that," I said, whipping the phone out of my pocket. Using Wyatt's encrypted program, I fired off a message. Under ordinary circumstances, I'd prefer to make these kinds of requests in person, but I couldn't take the time at this stage.

"You can get past it?"

"Probably, but I won't know for sure until the morning." I looked around, and spotted my coat draped across the back of a dining room chair. "I guess I should get going. I hope it's not a problem for your driver to come out so late."

"Oh, no. I can't make you go home after all this. I don't want you to have to wander home drunk," she said. I gave her a confused look and grabbed the coat, but I couldn't find a sleeve. "See? No, you can spend the night."

"What? I mean…" How could she just say it so directly? "No, I'd never be able to go along with that. It's not right to take advantage like that."

"Don't be silly. That bedroom's just sitting there empty every night. It won't hurt for you to stay there once." Fiona pointed off, vaguely in the direction of the guest bedroom.

"Oh, wait… you meant, uh—" I could feel my face growing redder by the second, and I could only hope she didn't have the wherewithal to notice. "Okay, fine. I'll stay."

"Alright. In that case, I'll see you in the morning," she said, planting a quick peck on my lips before retreating to the hallway between the two bedrooms. "Good night, Lance."

"Um, yeah. Good night," I managed to blurt out before she disappeared into the other room. I stood alone for a few minutes, trying to discern what Fiona could possibly have meant by that. Was it just the wine? Loosened inhibitions, liquid courage? I simply shook my head and walked into the guest bedroom for the night.

## **<u>Thursday</u>**

Dim sunlight filtered through the clouds as I woke the next morning. They flowed around the edges of the Arcology, passing by so close overhead that it seemed as though it might be possible to reach out and touch them. With clouds this low, it was only a matter of time before the pounding rains would resume their assault on the city.

I sat up, pleasantly surprised with a clear head and no hangover. I dressed and found Fiona sitting at the table, cradling her head in her hands. I could only assume she hadn't been so lucky.

"Good morning," I said, sitting down next to her. I rubbed a hand across my face, feeling the prickly stubble that had sprung up overnight. "You doing okay?"

"A little groggy, but I'll be fine." She looked up at me with a weak smile. "Have you heard back from your… contact? Is that what you'd call it?"

"I'm afraid not. It's pretty unusual." Typically, Wyatt's reply would be quick, regardless of how he decided. The messenger program was behaving strangely. "I may have to pay him a visit. If something went wrong and he didn't get my message, we can't afford to sit around waiting for nothing."

"Oh. I'm sorry if staying here last night left you in a bad spot."

"Don't be. I appreciated the chance to wake up with the sun for once," I said. "I'll have to get going soon, though. Can you call up the aerocar?"

"Sure." Fiona left the room for a moment, then returned with her phone. "Would you at least like to have some breakfast before heading off?"

"I'm sorry. I'll have to take a rain check on that." I grabbed my coat off the back of the chair and put it on. It was a very tempting offer, but with tonight as our last chance to act, I couldn't justify it to myself.

"I'll hold you to it," she said, handing my hat over as I headed out the door.

Within the hour, I was on the surface once again. The rain held off just long enough for me to get inside the bar, where I was met with an agitated stare from the bartender.

"What're you doing here? He doesn't have time for you today," he said, standing up behind the counter. He stared at me with dead eyes and a surly expression.

"Is that why he hasn't responded to me?" I asked, but he just kept staring. "Look, this won't take long. I just need to get one thing from him and then I'll be out of his hair. I don't have time to waste, either."

I tried to walk past the counter and down the hall towards Wyatt's den, but he stepped out to block me. I looked up at him, nose twitching as if he was suppressing a snarl. I pushed past, but he shot an arm out to stop me.

"Come on. What could possibly be so important? I bet this is just some kind of bizarre payback for implying he wasn't busy last time."

"I told you once. Now beat it." The bartender clenched his fist like he was waiting for me to try something. I wasn't about to fight Wyatt's friend, or whatever he is; he was far too big for me to take down, anyway.

"Wyatt! Come out here," I shouted. The bartender pushed me to the ground, hard.

"Quiet, you moron. We can't afford to have you here calling attention to the place." We both looked back behind him as the dull sounds of scraping metal rang out. The door opened, and Wyatt descended the stairs and turned the corner.

"Lance, what are you even doing here? I thought you were in Magmell," he said, gesturing for the bartender to back off. He did, and returned behind the counter. Wyatt walked over as I got to my feet.

"What the hell's gotten into him?"

"I can't take the time to explain what's up right now. Just trust me here, this is serious." Wyatt looked distracted, and tapped the side of his goggles. "No, what?"

He turned around and ran back up the stairs. I looked over at the bartender, who now didn't even so much as acknowledge my presence. I shrugged and followed him up the stairs.

"This won't take long, I promise. I just need a program that can dupe the keycard readers in Magmell. I have to gain access to the bulkhead areas by tonight," I said. He stared at the thin clear screens before him, their glow washed out by the light pouring in from the open door behind me.

"Seriously? You can find that for yourself. They're not that complicated," he replied without turning back. He typed a few lines and then started shuffling through the programs that hovered in front of him.

"Look, it's Magmell. I figured they'd be the highest quality security. Are you telling me any old signal hacking program will work?"

Wyatt sighed and flicked through a few more windows. He grabbed something and waved it over toward me. My phone buzzed to signal the queued up download.

"Alright, I'm going to make this quick. They just pushed a new patch for TerrainOS a few days ago. It broke a lot of things, but it's not mandatory yet. Last I checked, your phone had auto-update off. Am I right?"

"Yeah, it's still off. Is that why I couldn't contact you with the messenger you gave me?"

"Kind of. I can't explain now, but hold off on the update for as long as you can. If you let it update, that keycard spoofer won't run any more, and I won't be able to contact you, either." He turned around and looked me in the eye for the first time today. "You owe me for this. Big time. Now get going, and don't come back here until I give you the all clear."

Wyatt spun back around and resumed whatever he was doing. I watched him for a moment, waiting for something more, but he was already engrossed in the machine once again. Something about his actions left me distinctly unsettled.

"Fine, but you better explain later. Thanks for the program."

I closed the door behind me and left.

It was pouring by that point, so I called up a taxi and set off for home. I quickly studied the program on my phone, trying to familiarize myself with its functions. It seemed simple enough; I closed it, and the phone returned to its home screen, where Jerrod's note sat waiting. I figured that since I was already on the surface and my visit with Wyatt had been shorter than expected, it wouldn't hurt to take a little detour.

The taxi dropped me off at the south end of the Arcology, near one of the other gates. I walked in, and we went through the same rigmarole as a few days ago; the problem was that this time, I wasn't going to hand over my phone.

"I'm telling you, you don't want to take that in there," the guard said after I'd emptied my pockets of everything else.

"Well, I need it to deliver a message. I mean, you guys don't have any paper or anything like that around here, do you? I could copy it down, if you did."

"Gus, we got any paper here?" he asked. I knew they wouldn't, but that wasn't the real reason; I couldn't risk them snooping through it while I was gone and finding the keycard spoofer. The phone was locked down as much as possible, but I could never be sure it was enough.

"Of course we don't have any paper. I don't know if there's ever been any paper here."

"Then I'm going to have to take the phone in. Sorry," I said. The guard grunted and started flipping through his tablet.

"Alright, then. If that's the way you want it." He handed it over to me. "We're going to need biometric confirmation on the liability release. Anything you lose in there is on you, not us."

"I understand." I placed my hand on the pad, and let it take the necessary readings. "Sorry for the inconvenience, boys, but I've got a promise to keep."

"You're all clear, go ahead. Good luck hanging onto that thing. You're gonna need it." I stepped through the sally port, donned the respirator, and walked out into the base once more.

In the shadow of storm clouds, the Arcology somehow managed to be far more ominous. Without that bit of sunlight creeping in, the streets were only saved from the shadows by the small pools of light surrounding the street lamps. It made searching for the intersection of Q and 20 a nerve-wracking experience—every knocked over trash can, every lumbering shade in the distance could mean danger. Up in Magmell, travel by foot was looked down on, in spite of the beautifully maintained gardens; here, it was the only option, and it meant taking your life into your hands. I shuddered to think of a life where this constant state of fear was the norm.

Jerrod's family's building was easy enough to spot as I approached, graffiti scrawled on top of the large red markings that branded most tenements in the area. The interior was completely identical to the one Mrs. Warner lived in, only differing in the patterns left by years of accumulated filth. I knocked on the door number that Jerrod had given me, but there was no response. Again—nothing.

"Mrs. Carver, are you there?" I called out, echoing down the bare halls. "Mrs. Carver?"

"Whoever you are, go away. I'm not gonna speak to strangers," she said. This again? I could hardly blame the people here for being so cautious, but it certainly made things difficult.

"Mrs. Carver, I have a message from your son, Jerrod. I promised him I'd get it to you, so if you could please just open the door—"

"Nice try, but I won't be lettin' you in that easily." I heard some movement on the other side of the door, as if someone were trying to peer through the peephole. Trying to prove that I knew him seemed like my best bet.

"He told me that you moved here not long after the Arcology opened. Is that true?"

"Anybody could look that up."

"He also told me that he left to support you and the rest of the family after his father passed," I said. I'd hoped not to have to stir up old memories, but I didn't have much else to convince her with. "Please, Mrs. Carver. He was working for a group called Ascended Employment. Have you heard of them, at least?"

I could hear a younger female voice speak up quietly, just low enough to be indecipherable from this side. They whispered to each other for a moment, and after a brief deliberation, the locks clicked and it swung open. A feeble, gray-haired woman stood by the door as a teenage girl peeked her head around from behind it.

"My daughter believes you, so I'll give you a chance. Get in here, quick," she said, giving me the once over. I stepped inside, and the girl closed it behind me. "You sure don't belong down here, at the very least."

The Carver home was a bit nicer than Mrs. Warner's, but not by much. There were two sofas in the first room, and an extra bedroom that I assumed belonged to the kids. A pair of boys were seated on one of them, staring at a screen on the far wall that pumped out whitewashed corporate programming. Mrs. Carver shooed them off the sofa and stopped the show, waving me over.

"What'd you say your name was again?" I introduced myself and shook her hand, then sat down nearby.

"Can I get you something?" the girl asked. "We don't have any water right now, though. Jackson used up all our water allowance for the day in the bath."

She shot one of the boys a harsh look, to which he immediately began to protest. Mrs. Carver wasn't in the mood for bickering, however.

"All you kids get to your room. I'm going to need a moment with the man here." The girl looked annoyed, but led the two boys back and shut the door behind them. As soon as it was closed, she turned to me, her stern brown eyes staring straight through me. "Nina said she'd given Jerrod a flyer about those Ascended people. Are you saying he's working for them?"

"Yes, ma'am." I pulled the phone from my pocket. "If you'll allow me, I can show you his message on the screen there. It will all be clear."

She nodded, still distant. I opened his file and swiped it off toward the screen on the wall, where it started playing.

"Hi, mom. I don't have long, but I just wanted to say that there's no need to be worried about me, okay? I'm doing okay up here, but even when it does get rough, it's worth it knowing that it helps you. It's not so bad being someone's butler, and I actually get to see the Moon sometimes. Do you believe that? Still have to deal with clouds all the time, but it's pretty nice to look up at once in a while. Anyway, I hope things are a little better for you all now. I don't know when I'll get the chance to see you or send a message again, so I just wanted to say... I miss you. All of you. So pass my love on to Nina and Jackson and Marcus, okay? Goodbye."

The room was silent, and I could hear the scuffle of little

eavesdroppers against the closed bedroom door. Mrs. Carver stared at the screen, and I could just catch sight of a glimmering teardrop forming on her dark cheek.

"He's alive. I thought for sure, after so long—" she sniffled a bit and wiped the tear away. "He would be going on about the Moon when he's got so little time."

"You didn't know he was okay? Did you at least know that he left?" I asked. How could she not know he was alive and working? Unless…

"Nina told me after he left, but then a week passed, and then another, and we hadn't heard from him since. I was so sure that something happened to him on the way there, that I'd lost more family to those damn senseless gang fights…"

"Wait a minute. Are you telling me that you've never received the payment for his work up there?"

"Payment? If only. I haven't seen any outside income since the south end school was shut down," Mrs. Carver said. "We get the minimum level of income assistance, but that's it."

I didn't want to alarm her, but her answer had me concerned. "Your daughter was the one who told you, right? Could I speak to her for a moment?"

Mrs. Carver called her in, and she slipped through the bedroom door, careful not to let the boys escape. Nina stood there timidly, clutching at the folds of her long, worn skirt.

"Yeah, mom?" she said, taking in the mood of the room. Mrs. Carver waved towards me.

"Could you tell me where you learned about Ascended? Do you know anyone else who decided to take up their offer?" I asked. She glanced down at her feet. The straps on her shoes were busted, and she nearly lost them with each movement.

"My friend told me about it. Her father was planning to go to the meeting, so I got one of those flyers for Jerrod."

"Do you happen to know if her family has received any money from him, heard from him in any way?"

"I… I don't know. I haven't seen her in a while, and she never really liked to talk about it. Sorry."

"Is there any chance that I could speak to her?"

Nina nodded, and gave me their address, a few blocks away on R-16. "If you mention Ascended and tell her I asked you to visit her, she'll probably let you in."

"Thanks. I'll head over there right away," I said, rising to my feet. Mrs. Carver also stood up, slowly. She walked in a shambling manner, thoughts clearly elsewhere. All the way up in Magmell, no doubt. As we approached the door, she seemed to snap out of it for just long enough to see me off.

"I can't thank you enough for bringing this to me. I just hope I'll be able to see him again soon," she said. The bedroom door squeaked open, and Nina dashed off to tend to the boys once again.

"It's nothing. Goodbye, Mrs. Carver."

I donned the respirator once more and left the building. As I stepped outside, I saw a few young men, all wearing red, standing on the far corner and conversing quietly. They turned to look back as the door shut behind me, then dispersed. I pressed on, trying to ignore them as much as possible. After all, one wrong look was all it took down here.

Heading down to R, I found the area a little familiar but disorienting, like I was looking at it all from the wrong angle. I passed a pile of trash left for pickup two weeks too long; the respirator did nothing to help mask its overpowering stench of decay. A noise rattled out from behind, a scraping sound that sent a shiver through my spine. Not loud, but definitely no rat or feral dog. Footsteps?

I hesitated to turn, for fear of provoking whoever was responsible. Scanning the area ahead, I caught sight of two of the men from earlier, coming onto R from about two intersections further up. Much further than they could have gotten by walking. The pit of my stomach dropped like a rock from the top of the Arcology—they were trying to corner me. I picked up the pace a little, trying not to clue them in that I'd noticed. If I could just make it across the intersection, to the next building, I might be able to wait them out. Then again, they had all the time in the world.

I took in my surroundings, and my last desperate hopes were fading when I spotted a familiar plastic sign one block ahead from where the men were waiting. The food bank. A little farther away, but it was a far sight better than hoping they didn't follow me into a random building. I took off as fast as I could, a flat out run down the abandoned streets. This was one of those times where even I regretted my preference for fashion over function, as the coat definitely wasn't made for sprinting. My range of movement was a little restrained by the sleeves, and the tails of the coat kept getting in the way of my feet. The men behind me were running, shouting something I couldn't understand. Not English, or not entirely; it had a strong Spanish tone to it, at any rate. The ones ahead had started heading this way, too, and I caught a glimpse of a heavy section of metal pipe in one of their hands. They meant business. I was on the right corner now, maybe twenty feet from the door, and with any luck at all, I just might make it.

I'd already burned through all my luck for the week, however. I was tackled to the ground by one of the men from behind, and I kicked hard, trying to break loose. His buddies didn't take too kindly to that, and when I managed to roll over, two of them started kicking me in the ribs. I called out for help, hoping that Darren or anyone else might come out and scare them off. It was a long shot, with as deliberately vacant as the outside was, but it was my only chance. I tried to pull one of them down, thinking that maybe I could use him as a human shield to take some of the blows. That was about the point when the fourth member of their crew leaned down, real close, and grabbed my collar. His face was covered in beads of sweat, running down through a five o'clock shadow that wasn't particularly punctual. The tanned skin held the heavy remnants of amateurish tattoos, faded but still clearly visible. His right ear had a sizable chunk missing from it.

"You going to listen? Or should we get back to it?" he asked, breath heavy with a stench that managed to pierce the respirator's filter. He stared with the kind of crazy glint in his eyes that made me think he was really hoping for the latter. I nodded, figuring that was my best chance. "Take off the mask."

No choice—I slipped it off, and instantly began coughing as my lungs filled with the thick, polluted air. He snatched it away and stood up. One of the others yanked me upright and onto my feet. The one with the pipe held it with both hands, in the way that tough guys like to do when they're trying real hard to look the part. The scar through his eyebrow made it more convincing.

"Pockets. Empty them."

"The guards beat you to it. I don't have anything," I croaked between the hacking coughs. The air had a heaviness to it that was unlike anything I'd ever encountered. A smoke bomb would probably be easier to breathe in. I definitely wouldn't be able to fight anyone off like this, and yet I couldn't let them take the phone. There was too much important data on it, and with a little over a day left, I'd never be able to replace it in time to finish the case.

"Metro thinks he's funny." He flashed a fake smile and then socked me hard in the gut, leaving me doubled over. As if I needed any more trouble breathing. "Only warning you get. Do it." I didn't move, still doubled over and coughing. If I had literally anything else on me, I'd have offered it. He yelled it this time, "do it!"

The phone wasn't worth my life. I knew that. But even knowing it, all I could think of was that giving up the phone meant giving up on Melanie, on her mother. And that wasn't something I could bring myself to do; not at this stage.

"Felipe!" a voice behind me shouted. It had a scratchy tiredness to its tone that I recognized. "Lay off him. Please."

"This don't concern you, Darren. Get back inside," the man with the half-missing ear said. Darren walked up, just close enough that I could see him in the peripheries of my vision.

"This guy is helping me out. Please, I need him to find my girl." Darren turned to one of the other men, the one who'd tackled me. "Hey, Marco. It's been a while. How's your sister doing lately?" I couldn't see how he reacted, but he didn't say anything. "We got in some extra rations this week. If you stop by after close, I could give them to you for her."

A series of looks were exchanged between Felipe and the others. Finally, he gave a straight-faced nod, and then beckoned to the others and took off.

"You okay?" Darren asked as they left. A hacking cough was all I could manage in response. "Here, let's get back to the food bank. I really shouldn't leave it like this."

The food bank's lobby was crowded this morning, with dozens of people packed onto the benches and leaning on the walls. A young woman working the desk looked up as we entered and breathed a sigh of relief.

"I'm gonna need a minute still. Can you take care of this for now?" he asked, lifting the divider and waving me to follow him behind the counter. She grumbled momentarily and finally agreed. "I'll make it quick."

I followed him past the curtain and into the backroom, where he pulled up a box and gestured for me to sit down. It was a little easier to breathe in here, with the rattling ventilation system filtering out the worst of the pollution. Not every building down here was lucky enough to have one.

"Sorry they took your mask. I know it's tough for someone who's not used to the air to walk around without it, but if it makes you feel any better, there'll probably be some kid with asthma wearing it by Sunday."

"I hope that's the case, at least," I replied, taking a deep breath. The air was still rather dusty, but I could handle it.

"If that happens again, just do what they say. They wouldn't think twice about killing someone from the outer city."

"If I gave them my phone, it'd be nearly impossible to get Melanie back. Too much evidence on it."

"No backups?" he asked, and began digging around through the shelves. My phone was too modded to use the official backup systems; I couldn't risk the phone company finding out about it.

"Can't afford the service." That was true, too. "I take it you have something you want to tell me?"

"Sorry, I can't find our first aid kit. Someone must've taken it home again." I shrugged it off, slipping a hand under my coat to check my ribcage. Bruised, but not broken, thankfully. He sat down across from me, staring back with reddened and bloodshot eyes, rivers of crimson branching out from the iris like streams flowing down a mountaintop. "So after you left a few days ago, I decided to do a little looking around of my own. Talked to some of Melanie's friends, trying to find other people who went to work for that Ascended group. Finally found someone who used to work up there."

"I'm impressed. Not bad for three days." The kid might have some hidden talent for detective work. He leaned down, elbows on his knees.

"Well, what he had to say wasn't too good. He'd been working up there until about a month ago, when he got into a little dispute with his employer. Something got broken and he took the blame, although he swears he didn't do it. He was reported for trespassing and got tossed back down here. Gets home and — here's the kicker — his family got nothing," Darren said, sweeping his hand horizontally through the air. "Not one single paycheck for his whole time there. I found two others who said the same thing, too. The thing is, once they're back here, there's not a damn thing they can do about it. You can't get back in touch with your old boss. There's no one to go complain to, no one to fight for you. They're screwed."

"I was wondering how they'd get the funds to the people down here. I figured they'd pay them in Dyscoin or something, but I guess they just didn't bother at all." I looked around at the thin metal racks pressed up against bare concrete walls. Ripped and dented cardboard boxes lined the shelves, mishandled long before they ever reached the Arcology.

"I did find one person, who was in one of the first groups taken up by Ascended, that said he was paid in digital currencies. That only lasted for about three months, though. Then 'fees' started building up until there was nothing left." He sighed, and his fingers began to tighten around his knee. "I can't let that happen to Melanie. I hate to say it, but I don't know what more I can do. I couldn't even be sure if I'd get a chance to tell you what I'd found. It's so hard to get in touch with the outside."

"You've saved me a little legwork, Darren, so thanks for that. I'll do everything I can to help her." He nodded, then rose to his feet with the groan of a man twice his age. I stood as well, resting a hand on the shelf to guide myself up. As I did, I noticed just how many of the boxes were empty.

"I thought you said there were extra rations?" I asked, knocking on the empty cardboard. Darren shrugged.

"Being a little hungry for a week is a small price to pay for her safety," he said, and walked out of the back.

## **<u>Thursday Evening</u>**

I made it out of the Arcology without any further incident, although the guards did eye me suspiciously as I passed through without my mask. I headed home to get cleaned up and grab a few things. The cough was fading already, and I could only hope it'd be gone entirely before tonight. Lumbering into the bathroom, I examined myself in the mirror: some bruises were rising, and it wouldn't be pretty in a few days, but I'd live. Compared to the beating Marlowe took in *Farewell, My Lovely*, I was getting off pretty easy. I should just be glad I wasn't sapped.

I downloaded a copy of the Arcology's blueprints to help navigate the tunnels, and then gathered up some of my usual tools—lockpick, flashlight... and the pistol, resting comfortably in its drawer like a dragon sleeping in its cave, ready to expel its fiery slag at whomever crosses its path. I picked it up, felt the weight of the revolver in my hand. Its barrel was scratched, the grip worn smooth from decades of Grandpa's target practice. A . 38 Special, the kind of gun that everyone waved around in a film noir. A weapon as tied to its age as the fabled Excalibur was to King Arthur. But it held no mystique for me any more.

There wouldn't be anyone to make the decision for me this time, no guard to force me to leave it at the gate. The choice of whether to use it, to fire at someone again, would be mine and mine alone. The long gone echoes of a shattered window rang through my mind, but I shook it away. It wasn't just my safety at stake; Fiona would be right there in harm's way, too. I couldn't let that happen. If the cost of her safety was another weight on my conscience, then it was a small price to pay.

I pocketed the gun, gave her a call, and set off for the terminal.

Ruddy shafts of light broke through the clouds on my return to Magmell, signaling the fading sunlight. There wouldn't be much time to prepare. Fiona was once again waiting at the pad, and her expression shifted to one of concern as I climbed out of the aerocar.

"Lance! What happened to you?" she asked, reaching up to touch my face. Soft fingers, the kind that knew nothing of physical labor, stroked my cheek, but I moved her hand away. I didn't want to; even with the bruises, such a light touch sent shivers through my spine. I'd have loved nothing more than to relax and be nursed back to health by Fiona's gentle caress, but there was work to be done. The heavy pistol knocking against my thigh reminded me of that.

"It's fine. Just a little hiccup on the surface, nothing to worry about. Are you ready to go?"

She waved to the driver as he returned to the garage and turned back, her crimson hair glowing in the sunset. I couldn't quite read her expression through the glare, but her moment's pause made me wonder if perhaps she was reconsidering. I couldn't blame her if she was.

"Yeah. Let's get going."

I couldn't help but feel a little conspicuous as we walked the footpaths of Magmell once again, even though there were so few people about. The sun had just slipped below the horizon as the maintenance hatch came into view. Fiona leaned in to examine it.

"It's a little different than it used to be... but I was right, the lock's been broken again." She looked back at me with a quick smirk. "Where there's a will, there's a way."

Her hands searched around the outside of the hatch, until she found a loose bolt, which she carefully removed. One more, and I was able to wedge the door open. I retrieved the flashlight and aimed it into the darkness.

A handful of ladder rungs led down to a barren metal platform. I climbed down and was instantly overwhelmed by the scent of rust and booze. I took a moment to acclimate, then helped Fiona onto the platform. As I searched around with the flashlight, the ground sparkled and shone, like a field of green and amber fireflies. The walls had layers of graffiti on them, ranging from simple names and tags to a handful of crude sexual images, and even a few I recognized as corporate logos.

"You weren't kidding about the glass," I said. Fiona jumped down the foot or so from the platform to the tunnel's floor, and the glass crunched beneath her feet.

"Yeah. Doesn't seem to have been cleaned since I was here last," she said. She pointed down the tunnel, toward a small red light pulsing in the darkness. "That's the keycard reader."

I jumped down after her, and we walked to a chain link fence at the far end. Behind it was a second fence with solid metal bars as thick around as Fiona's wrist. We definitely wouldn't be able to get past without activating the reader. I took the phone out of my pocket and approached the light, emanating from a black square plate at waist height. Wyatt's keycard app opened and a message flashed across: "Testing Frequencies..."

A pleasant ding emerged from the phone, and the red light shifted to green. Physical locks pulled back, sending a weak echo down the tunnel. I handed the phone to Fiona and pulled the gate open. We stepped through it and stared out into the pitch black tunnel before us. There were lights installed, but without a maintenance kit, we had no way to turn them on. The gate slammed shut; no turning back now. The tunnel wasn't quite wide enough for us to walk side by side, so I took the flashlight and led the way.

Walking down this quiet, empty hall, it felt as though the walls were pushing in with each step. My shoulders brushed up against the cold, unpainted steel as I stepped over exposed pipes and ducked under electrical conduits.

"The blueprint shows it opening up soon. There's a big space around the central support column," Fiona said. A faint glow appeared at the far end of the tunnel, shifting the darkness to a slightly lighter shade. As we drew closer, the source of the light became clear—open space surrounded the pillar, leaving a few feet between it and the surrounding catwalk. It passed through the ceiling of the underside, which had no such opening, and on up to the top of the tower. It was a junction, with several other tunnels also converging on this point. Fiona walked carefully to the edge, and we looked down onto the level below.

It was quite a majestic sight: the gardens and fields were well lit by specialized grow-lights, and their grids and rows were visible across the entire floor, sorted by type. Robotic sprinklers glided from line to line, spraying the crops with water from their vast reservoirs of filtered rain.

"I've never seen the farming levels in person before. It's fascinating, in a way," she said, leaning over the railing. Her necklace dangled precariously above the void, spinning back and forth as if taunting gravity with its thin, twisted chain. "If only the rest of the Arcology could have been so successful."

"The worst part is that there's really no reason it couldn't be," I replied, my eyes glued to the machinery surrounding the pillar's base. I could hear the wind rushing by below, its soft whistling sound emanating from the catwalk's grated surface. The distance to the ground grew more apparent with each passing moment. "Let's get going."

We navigated the narrow walkway, all the while trying not to acknowledge the hundred foot drop beneath us. I moved slowly, each step accompanied with a tight grip on the railings that were just a bit too low for comfort.

"Are you afraid of heights?" Fiona asked.

"Don't be ridiculous. I'm just being cautious." Of course, I couldn't help but look down once again, and grasped the railings all the tighter as the anxiety built up. I'd almost swear the catwalk was swaying in the winds.

"Right…" she said, stepping forward. I took a deep breath and lifted my eyes from the surface. Just don't think about it. It's no different than walking down there would be. With a steady pace, I managed to reach the end of the catwalk. Once I'd set foot on the solid metal flooring, I backed away from the ledge as far as I could, leaning back onto the wall. My heart was pulsing rapidly, booming throughout every part of my body. I exhaled slowly, hoping desperately that this would be the worst of it. Fiona stepped up onto the platform without looking and fidgeted with the phone.

"Alright, this is the tunnel that passes under the house where I met Jake. It leads into the wider underside, where the water and power utilities are located. It shouldn't be hard to find the training camp from there, since there doesn't appear to be anywhere else you could keep a large group of people," she said. She looked up from the phone and I immediately stood upright. "Do you need a minute?"

"No, I'm ready. Let's go," I replied, adjusting my hat and straightening my coat. She smiled sweetly, a compassionate gleam in her eyes, and we resumed our trek.

The tunnel wasn't long, and the bright, noisy maintenance area ahead gave us a clear destination instead of murky darkness. It ended suddenly in a large, warehouse-like space, with wide supports regularly spread around the floor. The ceiling was a maze of pipes and wires, each one leading to a mansion or streetlight or fountain above. The room had a triangular shape to it, walls angled outward from the tunnel's mouth; it had to be at least an eighth the size of the whole level. Rows of massive power relays and water pumps stood before us, roaring obnoxiously and blocking our view. I walked up and peered out from behind it. The area seemed to be totally vacant, but the far right corner was dark, and from what I could make out, separated from the rest by large sheets hanging from the ceiling beams as dividers.

"I think I see the camp," I said to Fiona, but she couldn't hear over the machinery. I pointed to the dark corner, and darted forward to the next relay. She paused for a moment, then followed. As we crept ever closer to the camp, the relays gave way to pumps, and the noise gradually died down. I could see two pairs of men standing along each of the outer dividers, watching for prying eyes or breakout attempts. I scanned the area, looking for some path that might grant access to the camp. There wasn't one, but a breaker panel a few yards back caught my eye. We crept over to it, and I signaled to Fiona to keep watch.

"What are you doing?" she asked over her shoulder.

"Hopefully providing a distraction," I replied. The panel was bolted shut with an old physical lock, the standard sort that was just simple enough. I shuffled through my pockets until I found the lockpick, nestled away in my coat. Within moments the lock clicked open, and the breakers were laid out before me, nicely labeled. The switch for the right corner was already flipped; the lock had to have been put there by Ascended. I flipped the switch for the opposite corner, and the remainder of the far end fell into darkness.

"The guards look confused," Fiona said, then pulled back behind the nearest machine. I locked the breaker box and joined her. "I think they're coming this way to check it out."

"This is our chance, then," I said, sliding up a few rows to the next pump. I waved Fiona over, and we ducked down on the side nearest to the wall. The guards' approach was just barely audible over the humming of the generators. I pressed a finger to my lips as Fiona looked up.

"Why do we have to be the ones to fix it?" one of the guards asked as they walked by.

"Just shut up. I'm tired of listening to you complain all the time. Why are you even here if you hate it so much?" the other answered. It sounded like they'd come to a halt.

"Because I needed some booze money. My stupid parents want every dollar I spend accounted for."

"Fine. I'll buy you a whole case tomorrow if you can make it through the rest of the night without whining."

"Deal," the first said. They resumed walking, and I let them put some distance between us before I signaled to Fiona to start moving once more.

The darkness provided enough cover for our approach, and we reached the divider without incident. They reminded me of stage curtains, drawn loosely at the end of a show. I lifted the bottom off the ground and we crawled underneath. I rose to my feet and relaxed a bit; the guards wouldn't be able to spot us from here.

"Okay, Fiona, turn on—" I whispered, but approaching footsteps cut me off. I slipped into the folds of the divider with her in tow, pulling it shut around us. I could hear a set of footsteps coming closer, and the area lit up from a flashlight's beam. It was quiet here, with the divider muffling what little mechanical noise could still be heard on this end.

"All clear on this end," a voice called out. The other swung the flashlight's beam around, checking further. Fiona and I were pressed close together, my arms wrapped around her to keep us from being exposed. It certainly wasn't how I'd imagined getting to hold her for the first time.

I tried to keep the folds together just tightly enough to hide us without looking suspicious. A few excruciating seconds of silence passed before I heard footsteps moving away. I let go of the curtain and we spilled out into the hall. We both breathed a sigh of relief.

"Well, at least we know where the other two guards are now," she said, as softly as possible. I nodded and straightened my coat, then cut the flashlight back on.

"Start recording with the phone, so we can at least get some evidence." I knelt down on the floor and peaked under the next divider. The coast was clear, so I crawled under, with Fiona following behind. It looked like a storeroom, filled with large stacks of cheap, long lasting foods, the same kind as in Darren's food bank. We ducked under two more dividers until coming across a group of girls lying on the floor. Several of them sat up, squinting in the light. Fiona placed a finger to her lips and kept them quiet, and I pointed the flashlight at the curtain to minimize any stray light that might give us away.

"It's okay. We're here to take you home," Fiona said. She panned the phone camera over the group.

"What? I don't want to go back," one of the girls replied, rising to her feet. "I chose to come up here."

"You did, and we know that, but you weren't given all the facts," I said. I stepped forward a little, and a head poked out under the divider from the opposite side. I waved the young man in, and soon others followed. "You've been lied to. Ascended isn't going to provide the help you've been told they will. I've heard from those that have come before you, who returned to the bottom only to find that they hadn't been paid at all—their employers felt the privilege of living up here was payment enough. All that time up here was for nothing; you can't help your families like that."

"I don't give a shit about helping anyone else. I'm here for myself. There's no way living here can be worse than down there," another man said, ducking under the divider from the next room.

"I'm sure you know it's illegal to work like this, but have you thought about the consequences of that? You have no one to go to if you're mistreated, no way to escape if you decide to quit. Your boss can threaten you with expulsion at any time, for even the most minor of offenses. It's exploitation, plain and simple. Will you just hope that the person who decides to hire you is a nice one? Nice people don't hire illegal servants in the first place."

There were a few murmurs in the crowd, and more people were sneaking under the divider to see what was happening. Fiona had the camera phone pointed squarely at me. The tide of the room was shifting, and I decided to continue.

"Think about how you've been treated so far, on the way here. How you're living now, sleeping on the floor with a dozen others in a glorified tent. You've sacrificed a lot, I know, trying to provide for people back home. I've spoken to the people working now and they've told me what it's like. No one asks their names or treats them like human beings. They never get to contact their families, so they have no way of knowing if their efforts are actually helping. Could you imagine being thrown out after working here for a year, only to find out your family had received nothing whole time?"

The crowd burst out into whispers once again. It was time to pull out the trump card Fiona had learned of last night.

"And it gets worse. Ascended isn't planning to stop with just maids and butlers and landscapers. They want to move into other areas, to take their exploitation to the next level. They're going to start pressuring you into prostitution next. Is that what you came up here for? Because when they have all the power, it won't take much. You agree to it or it's back to the bottom. And it won't stop there. What will it be after that? Drug smuggling? Who knows what they'll be asking of you in a few years' time—if you even make it that long."

"It's true," a girl in a stained blue nightgown said. She climbed to her feet and continued, "that balding man… he already tried to talk me into it. I know I'm not the only one, either."

Their chatter grew louder, and I was starting to get worried about attracting attention.

"What if I still don't want to go? You gonna force me back?" the man retorted. The area fell silent again.

"What's your name? If you don't mind me asking."

He stared at me, confused and suspicious, until finally he said, "Martin."

"No, Martin, I'm not going to force you to come with me. You have the facts now, it's your choice. But we are going to do everything we can to put a stop to this exploitation, even if that means putting a stop to the whole operation." I laid it out as firmly as I could. I hadn't expected to meet anyone who would be okay with working for Ascended after hearing all of that, but I wasn't here to kidnap people.

"If you come with us now, we can get you back to your families, and then we'll make sure none of you can be used like this again," Fiona said. The crowd grew louder and louder, and I was sure the guards would come investigating if it kept up.

"We have to get moving. If you want to go home, then keep it down and get ready. We don't have long," I said. People ducked back under the dividers and the noise died off. I walked over to Fiona, who shut the recording down and handed the phone back. Before I had a chance to speak to her, a young woman in a tattered nightgown interrupted us.

"I was talking to Dana and she said you're the man she saw last night, the one who was working for my mother. Is that true?" she asked.

"Are you Melanie Warner?" I asked. She did look a little like the girl in the picture, but older, more tired and worn out.

"Yeah, that's me," the girl replied. Fiona and I exchanged a quick glance. "Do you... have any news about her?"

"She's very worried about you; had no idea where you'd gone. She actually managed to break out into the city looking for help."

Melanie shook her head, and a little smirk appeared. "Wow, I guess she's still got those nerves of steel after all." It faded slowly, and after a brief pause, she said, "I was going to leave her a note, but I—I just couldn't figure out what to write. I knew there was no way she'd go for it. I was kinda hoping that she'd get the picture after my first paycheck arrived. Just thinking how she'd feel if she never got one..."

"No one would know about this if it weren't for her tenacity," Fiona said. Melanie gave a somber nod.

"Melanie, can you help us coordinate the others? I'm sure you know them better than we do," I asked. I wanted to give the girl a moment, but every second that ticked by was one more chance to get caught.

"Right, yeah. I can help with that," she said, running her fingers through her hair. "Um... Ascended, they don't seem to have a whole lot of people working for them. I think I've only seen like eight people so far. Most of the time, they're back in a tunnel back that way, in the corner near here. It's right below that house where you spoke to Dana, know what I mean? There's usually a guard or two in the other corner, but that's it. There's not much set up back there, so it should be the easiest way out of here."

It seemed like our best chance, since the way we came was no longer an option. Still, it was a long way around the circumference of the Arcology.

"What's going on in here?" a voice shouted. I winced, and many of the girls in the room dropped to the floor immediately. I looked around, but there were no guards in here; it had to have come from one of the adjoining shelters.

"Fiona, keep them calm. You and Melanie get these other groups ready. I'll go investigate," I said. She nodded and led Melanie down into the crowd. I reached into my coat and checked for the gun; still there. As I approached the divider to the left, I could hear the guards arguing with the men over there. It sounded like they were standing just inside the entrance.

I moved carefully to the doorway and peered around the

corner. The hall was completely empty, but I could just barely see the guard's reflected light coming from the opened curtains next to me. I crept into the hall, stopping just a few feet away; only the divider separated us.

"What, you guys thinking of wandering off? Going on a little walk, eh?" the guard said. Hearing the voice from this close, it was definitely the same guard that had been checking before.

"I don't think that would work out too well for them. Might lose their jobs, get sent back to the bottom. You wanna go back to the bottom?" another added. The sounds of fabric rustling and a slight thump came through the divider.

"Yes," a worker answered.

"You hear that? He's barely been up here for a week and already getting homesick. Hate to break it to you, kid, but it's too late to go back home. You have a contract with us, after all."

"Your contract's only good if you follow through on it, too."

Both guards laughed, and I could hear a small scuffle on the other side of curtain.

"You didn't read very closely, did you?" The first guard said, so quiet that I could barely make it out. He followed that up loudly with, "don't you worry about that."

The scuffling increased and I knew I had to act. I took a deep breath, gathered my courage, and charged into the room.

I was able to catch the guards by surprise, tackling the closest to the ground. His flashlight clattered to the floor along with us, rolling away and throwing the room into darkness. The guard scrambled for something I couldn't see. I grabbed the back of his collar and lifted his head up, then slammed him to the floor. He tried to roll over, and it was only when one of the workers grabbed the flashlight that I was able to see the pistol at his side. I dropped an elbow to his gut, and he wheezed loudly. His left fist caught me in the chest, pushing me back onto his right arm and pinning it to the floor. I held it there as best I could, desperately struggling to get to the pistol on his leg first. One of the workers gave him a rough kick to the head, knocking him out cold. The man with the flashlight ran up beside me. I was able to pull the gun from its holster and pointed it at the first guard, who was now being attacked by the kid he'd been bullying and several others. They held him back, providing a clear target, and I could see the fear on his face as he stared down the muzzle of a gun for the first time. That same fear I'd known in Overton's office.

"Hold him there. Take his gun." The kid grabbed it and walked over. I took it and slipped it into my pocket.

"Hey, whoa, don't shoot. I don't know who you are or what's going on. I'm just a maintenance guy. They said they'd pay me a grand to watch these guys so I did," he rambled. I looked him over, mussed hair and wrinkled coveralls. Then I noticed the golden shine of a watch, just barely sticking out past the cuff of his sleeves.

"You don't want to get shot, I don't want to shoot you. So just cooperate." I walked over to him and pulled the sleeve back, confirming my suspicions. It was an expensive watch, one that no maintenance man could afford. "Maintenance guy, right. Shut up and get over there with your buddy."

He looked dismayed, and the men holding him slowly relaxed their grip and backed off. I kept the gun on him as he walked over and sat down next to the other guard.

"You guys have anything we can tie them up with?" I asked the man with the flashlight. He looked around a bit, and one of the other men crawled under the divider. He returned a few moments later, holding half a dozen ropes of various lengths.

"From the food pallets," he said, handing them off. Another worker looped the ropes around the guards' hands and feet and tied them off together tightly.

"Let's find the other groups and get going," I said, gesturing to the flashlight man. He nodded, and we left the guards helpless in the middle of the room.

"One second," the kid said. He yanked the curtain that had acted as the door down, then threw it over the guards. I led the group out, then looked over my shoulder just in time to catch the kid smacking the guard in the head one last time. He saw me and responded only with a toothy grin that said it all. I shook my head and left.

We met up with Fiona and the girls from next door right as Melanie returned with the other groups. Fiona seemed a little shocked by the gun in my hand, so I put it away.

"Is this everyone who wants to go?" I asked Melanie as she approached.

"Yeah. It's about two-thirds of us," she replied. "The rest aren't interested in leaving."

"I guess that's all we can do for now. Let's get moving. It'll be hard to travel quietly with this many people, so the sooner, the better."

"Do you think the ones we leave behind will cause a problem?" Fiona asked.

"There's no way to be sure, but we can't do much about it either way. Let's just hope we can get out before anyone notices," I said. I took out my phone and pulled up the blueprints. It looked like the tunnel across from here would eventually lead back to the other side, but it'd be a long walk. "You said there's usually a guard in the opposite corner, right?"

"Right," Melanie said. "They don't have much presence over there aside from that."

"Okay. Get everyone lined up, I'll take a look outside." I took off for the outer walls of the camp and looked across to the far side, which was still shrouded in darkness. I could make out a few of the pillars along the edge of the lights, but beyond that it was indistinguishable. I glanced back towards the pumps and saw that the other two guards were still a ways off, but I couldn't tell if they were making their way back yet.

I returned to the hallway and found everyone had been

gathered up into four lines, with Fiona talking to Melanie out front.

"How many people do we have?" I asked as I joined them.

"Thirty-seven workers, plus the two of us," Fiona replied. Getting this many people around is always difficult, but doing it without attracting attention is nearly impossible.

"Alright, let's head off to that tunnel. Get everyone single file. We'll walk as close to the outer wall as we can. Melanie, can you take the rear, make sure no one gets lost?" I said.

"Yeah, I can do that." Melanie had a hidden talent for managing groups of people, it seemed, and we had them ready in no time. Fiona and I took the lead, carefully guiding the group out from behind the dividers.

I was pleasantly surprised as we walked through the shadows along the wall; the group was quiet enough that I could hear the droning of the pumps from here. Looking out into the lit portion, I could see the far wall was coming up, but there was still no sign of the guard Melanie had warned of. Perhaps he'd wandered off when the lights went out, or maybe he already knew about our little jailbreak and had gone out for reinforcements.

I spotted a white glow emanating from behind one of the supports, and signaled for the group to stop. I reached into my pocket and placed a hand on the pistol grip. Fiona watched, dismayed, but I couldn't risk him getting the upper hand; not with her around. I crept closer until I reached the pillar, then stepped out from behind it, pointing the gun straight at him. He looked up from his phone and his jaw dropped. I gestured for him to be quiet.

"Whoa, there. I'm just playing with my phone, I don't want any part of this," he whispered. I extended my hand, pointing to the gun at his side.

"I'll be taking that."

"Alright, here," he replied, fumbling around a bit until he could undo the holster with one hand. He slowly offered the gun and I pocketed it. He stood there agape, his face made grotesque by the brilliance of the phone shining up from below. His eyes twitched back and forth, examining my face.

"Get down."

He complied, but there was still a hint of spite in his movements. The phone's screen dimmed as he settled onto the floor.

"I'll need that, too," I said. I couldn't risk him calling for backup.

"Ah, come on. I just got this two weeks ago. It'll take forever to replace all the identification and crap. I won't call anyone. Just let me keep it," he whined. I knelt down, the pistol held loosely in my hand, mere inches from his face. He huffed and handed it over. "Fine. I'll report it stolen or something, I guess."

I took it and aimed the light back at him. There wasn't any more rope, and I couldn't very well drag him along at gunpoint the whole way.

"Get out of here. Do not talk to anyone else, or your phone won't be the only thing you lose tonight," I said, waving him off with the gun barrel. He got up, shot me a dirty look, and took off towards the lit area at a steady pace. Here's hoping it was a halfway decent bluff.

I examined the door he should have been guarding, which had another keycard lock. I beckoned to Fiona using the light on the phone, and she brought the group with her.

"He ran off pretty quickly. Are you sure that's okay?" she asked.

"I just scared him a little. He's not going to be calling anyone down." I handed her the guard's phone, and she passed it off to Melanie, who studied it with the kind of reverence typically reserved for national treasures. I got out my own and opened the keycard app, but the code from before wouldn't work. I reset it and tried again. The "Testing Frequencies…" appeared once more, and it isolated a different one this time. "Looks like they reprogrammed the locks on this side to work for them."

"Better thank your friend, then," Fiona said. I responded only with a mildly annoyed grunt. The door slid open, and I went through to scout it out. It was a small tunnel, scarcely wider than the door, with fluorescent lights spaced far apart down the length. I consulted the blueprints as Fiona stepped through and joined me.

"It looks like this opens up after a while, and eventually reaches a landing bay for maintenance and supply drop off," I said. "This is going to take a lot longer than I thought. Every minute we're up here is just one more chance for something to go wrong."

"Hang on, let me try something..." she handed me the flashlight, then pulled her phone out of her pocket. "I just barely have a signal, but it might be enough."

"What are you doing?"

"Just wait a minute and see." She tapped the screen and held the phone up to her ear, meandering down the tunnel as she did. "Hi there, Benny. I have a bit of an unusual request, but I can assure you, it'll be worth your while."

Who could she possibly be calling right now? I waited, rather impatiently, until she wandered back this way.

"You can do that, then? Excellent. Thank you so much. See you soon," Fiona said, then hung up. She slipped the phone back into her pocket. "Alright, Lance. All we have to do is get them to that drop off point. Everything should be taken care of after that."

"What? What did you just do?"

"I called my driver. He's going to come around here and pick us up."

"That car can hold four people, max. What about everyone else?"

"You'll see," she said. I decided to leave it be and returned to the door. The group outside was growing restless, so I called them in and we set off for the landing bay.

As if our earlier walk through the tunnels hadn't been bad enough, traversing the narrow paths with dozens of people in tow added a whole new level of misery to it. It became hot and humid fast, and the smell was overwhelming. I'd hoped we could leave it behind as we pushed forward, but it didn't seem to help much. It was more or less impossible to speak to anyone else without stopping the entire procession. I realized then that this was only a small taste of what these people had gone through to get up here—fueled by hope, and duty, and desperation, but more than that, love.

The dim lighting was taxing, and their steady fluorescent trembling didn't help. The slight curve of the tunnel effectively hid everything ahead from view, and taken in combination with the featureless metal walls and lights made it feel as though we'd stumbled upon a mythical labyrinth from which there was no return. Fiona seemed to be holding up okay, and most of the group was treating it like this was an everyday occurrence, so I certainly wasn't about to complain.

It was at this point that I felt a welcome draft of fresh air, trickling down to announce the approaching exit. The tunnel's mouth came into view not long afterward, growing larger and brighter as we drew near. At last, I set foot outside, onto a raised platform only a few feet wide that ran around the perimeter of the landing bay. The clouded sky was backlit by a full moon, just barely illuminating the entrance.

"Great," Fiona said, checking her phone for the time. "He should be here any minute now."

I was still trying to figure out how exactly Fiona's driver would be able to just fly in here and pick everyone up when a shadow fell over us. A massive aerocar had risen up alongside, its vague borders stretching out past the walls of the landing bay. It was a luxury bus, designed to ferry groups of visiting businessmen and politicians to the top of the Arcology for vanity tours. It sidled up to the building as close as it could get, then sent out a short ramp to bridge the gap. The doors opened, and Fiona's driver was standing there, waving us in.

"The wind's not too bad tonight, but I wouldn't risk it by taking your time," he shouted over the bus's fans.

I looked back at the group, staring in wonder at the enormous vehicle before us.

"Well, you heard him. Start boarding, and don't look down. Just concentrate on getting across, and once you're aboard, head to the back," I said. They walked up, and the line slowly made its way onto the bus. Things moved smoothly at first, until one young man found himself at the front of the line. He stepped forward and glanced down to check his footing, catching an eyeful of the city streets below. He jumped back immediately, scurrying away from the edge. His eyes were glued to the platform, and he ran his fingers through his hair and across his colorless face.

"I can't. It's so small, and so high… the wind! I don't want to fall." He sat close to the floor and grasped his knees. I could hardly blame the man; I wouldn't have been too eager to cross the ramp myself, but it was time to sink or swim.

"Hey, listen. Can you hear me?" Fiona asked, leaning over slightly. The man gazed up and nodded. "You can do this. Look, it's only a few feet. You can walk a few feet in a straight line, can't you? You could walk that ramp with your eyes closed."

"Don't be ridiculous."

"You do it all the time, don't you? Walking is totally natural. You walked all the way here without falling over, after all. What's the difference between that and the ramp?"

"It's way more dangerous, for starters," he replied, sitting upright. The driver was standing impatiently, and tapped his wrist when I looked over at him.

"Come on. You've got this. I'll hold your hand on this end, and the driver can take your hand on the other end. You'll have someone to help keep your balance the whole time."

He looked up, and the driver extended his arm. Fiona reached out and took the man's hand, and he rose, trembling, to his feet.

"Just take a deep breath and step," she said.

"Deep breath..." the man repeated. He set one foot on the ramp, and put his other arm out for balance, imitating a tightrope walker. Another step, and he reached forward to take the driver's hand. Hesitantly, his grip on Fiona's hand weakened, and at last he was on the ramp. The driver pulled him forward, one step at a time, until he made it inside.

"See? No problem," Fiona shouted over to him. The man looked back, his face slowly relaxing from its tense and frightened state. As a smile appeared, the driver moved him toward the back of the bus, and the next person stepped up.

I glanced over at Fiona, who was still assisting people up onto the ramp. I was amazed at how calm and supportive she could be, even at a time like this. She caught me looking and gave a little smile before the next person stepped up.

It didn't take long after that for nearly all of the passengers to board. As the last few made their way up, the driver leaned out the door, standing on the edge of the ramp.

"This thing's only rated for thirty passengers max. I know it can take at least thirty-five, but I don't think it's wise to push it much past that," he said. I looked over at Fiona. "Sorry, but it was the biggest thing I could get."

"Looks like you and I have some walking to do, then," I said to her. She nodded stoically, and we pushed the last few people on until Melanie was the only one that remained.

"Melanie, wait," I said, just as she moved up. "We're going to present our evidence against Ascended to the authorities up here, and it might be helpful to have some firsthand testimony. Would you be willing to go with us tomorrow?"

"Oh... but wouldn't that be a problem? I mean, where would I hide out until then?"

"You can stay with me for the evening. It won't be a problem," Fiona answered. Melanie was a little taken aback.

"With you? Up here? Like, a nice place?"

"Well, yes..."

"I—okay, yeah. I'll talk to them with you," Melanie said. Her eyes were a little wide, as if the implications of it all were dawning on her.

"Excellent," I said. I leaned in towards Fiona a little bit and whispered, "thanks for doing this. I know it's a little much."

"Don't worry about it," she whispered back. She waved to the driver, and he returned to the driver's seat, retracted the ramp, and took off.

"Where's he going to take them?" Melanie asked as the bus descended out of view.

"They're going to the aerocar terminal, and from there they'll take taxis back to the base of the Arcology," Fiona replied. It was quiet now, with only the sound of the winds whipping past. I pulled up the blueprints once more, double checking our route.

"Are we ready to head on?" I asked. "It's going to be a long trip back, and it's already late."

"Right. Let's get going," Fiona said, stepping into the tunnel. I was about to do the same when a sudden echoing sound from behind drew my attention. I looked back at the tunnel we'd come from and caught the gleam of a flashlight coming into view.

"Oh shit."

# **Thursday Night**

I pushed Fiona and Melanie deeper into the tunnel. At the very least, they had to get away. I reached into the pocket of my coat and passed each of them a guard's pistol.

"Go, run!" I said. "They're coming after us and you don't want to be here when they catch up."

"What? What about you?" Fiona asked. She held the gun with two fingers, in a disgusted manner. This had to be the first time she'd ever touched one.

"Don't worry about that. Go."

"Don't move!" A voiced called out from the other side. "That goes for everyone."

So much for keeping Fiona and Melanie out of trouble. I stepped in front of them and put my hands up.

There were at least half a dozen of them, and as they stepped out into the drop off area, I recognized the first as the kid with the phone, followed by two other guards. Guess I need to work on my poker face.

The weaselly man I'd seen in the basement emerged next, and then Jake, whose face was a portrait of barely restrained fury even from here. It wasn't until the last person appeared that I was really thrown for a loop—it was Nick, staring across at me with an equal amount of disbelief.

"It's you! The one who was hanging around Fiona. Jay, or whatever," he shouted, and Jake looked over at him in surprise. I remembered what she'd said after the meeting last night and silently cursed our luck. Things were complicated enough already.

"You know this guy?" Jake asked, and Nick nodded. He seemed only a hair more sober than he had been on Tuesday night.

"He's that little prick I was telling you about, the one at the ball with her a few days ago."

"That's a bit strong, don't you think? We barely even spoke, after all," I said. Nick's eyes narrowed as a devious grin crept across his tanned face.

"Oh, just wait till Fiona hears about this," he replied. Jake stared at me, and the recognition finally clicked.

"Yeah... I remember. You were at the ball the other night. I knew there was something off about you. Now, step aside and bring your little friends out with you." The guards leveled their guns at me, and for a moment I considered making a move for my own, but even now I wasn't sure that I could bring myself to use it. I moved over a few feet, allowing them to exit the tunnel. As Fiona set foot into the dim and scattered moonlight, Nick's jaw hit the floor.

"Fiona? What? What are you doing here?" Nick shouted. He took a step forward and Jake shot his arm out, holding him back.

"I'm putting a stop to this. It's wrong and it has to end," she replied, grasping the pistol grip so tight that her knuckles were turning white. The barrel was pointed at the floor, jittering in that telltale adrenaline-fueled manner.

"Put your guns down, ladies. You're clearly not going to use them," Jake said. Both of them looked to me, and I nodded. They set them on the floor. "Now, where are the others you took?" Nick kept yelling over him, his speech growing more slurred with his concentration broken.

"Fiona, this is ridiculous. Get over here."

"I'm not going anywhere with you, Nick. Not now, not ever."

Her voice was harsh, almost cruel. So unlike the person I'd gotten to know. "I can't deal with you any more. I've had it. I left because I didn't want to be that kind of person any more. To know that you were capable of being a part of this kind of sick, twisted exploitation… it scares me to think what I'd have become if I stayed with you."

"What are you talking about? They wanna work, I want somebody to work for me. What's the problem?"

"Can you finish this later?" Jake asked Nick through gritted teeth. He faced me and asked again. "Where are the others?"

"They're long gone," I replied. "You won't be able to get them back, and pretty soon everyone down there will know the truth. It's over."

"Don't lie to me, Nick. I know all about how you treat your servants. Throw any bottles at them lately? I hear it's become your favorite pastime."

"I never threw—I mean, I don't remember throwing…" Nick pointed at me. "You! This is all your fault, isn't it? If it weren't for you, Fiona would still be—"

"Shut up, Nick," she said, cutting him off. "The only reason I even spoke to you again was to put a stop to this. There was never a chance I'd go back."

He fell silent, for once, staring off at the ground. His hands had a frantic desperation to them, as if he was struggling to make sense of it all.

"You owe me quite a bit of money, then," Jake said, ignoring them. "How do you plan to repay that?"

"Don't you have enough money?" I asked. "What could you possibly be gaining from this? Skimming those servants' paychecks, it has to be chump change for someone living up here. Why? Couldn't hack it at a real business?"

"Business enterprises, criminal enterprises. They're both the same. I'd hoped this would be a little more exciting, what with the added challenge of keeping it under the radar. But it's every bit as dull right now," he replied. "It's the same basic rules. I saw a niche and I filled it. Supply and demand. They all volunteered for it."

"You going to claim they volunteered for harassment and prostitution, too?" The clouds parted a little, and flat gray moonlight streamed in under the overhang. Nick looked up, his face emotionless as the pieces came together.

"Their lives down there were already pathetic. Nothing that could happen to them in Magmell would even come close." Jake's voiced turned harsh. "Your meddling is what will cause them to suffer."

"You keep telling yourself that." I stared him down. Melanie stood close behind me, grasping onto the sleeve of my coat. I wished I could give it to her; she had to be cold standing here, with only a thin nightgown to protect her from the wind. Jake laughed and elbowed the weaselly man in the arm.

"This guy likes to act tough. Is that why you look like you're three months early for Halloween?" The weaselly man snorted a little. I hoped they'd keep believing it.

"Better than abusing people because you can't get out of Daddy's shadow."

A ferocious scowl appeared on Jake's face, but only for an instant. He stretched his arms out and transformed it into a yawn. "I've had enough of this. What do you think we should we do? I'd say just shoot them, but people will start asking questions if your ex goes missing."

The weight of the gun in my coat pocket knocked against my body in the wind, reminding me of its presence. It was all coming down to that again. I didn't want to be forced to shoot at someone again, to see the life drain from their eyes like blood from the wound. I wouldn't be able to live with myself; I knew that now. But it wasn't about me. The thought of something happening to Fiona, of Mrs. Warner waiting endlessly for Melanie's return, never truly knowing what happened to her...

maybe I'd just have to find a way.

"Whoa, whoa, wait a minute. What? You can't kill Fiona," Nick said, placing a hand on Jake's shoulder. He turned him until they were face to face.

"Well, what do you want me to do? She knows too much about this now. We already know she doesn't like it."

Nick stared at him in disbelief. It seemed like he'd finally found a line he wasn't willing to cross. And if I'd learned anything from Sam Spade, it was to promote dissent among the enemy whenever possible.

"I thought you liked Fiona, Nick. All those nights of partying, quiet moments in your piano room... are you going to let him do that to her?" I said. He glared my way momentarily, then back to Jake. I kept my eyes on the guards, so I couldn't see it, but I heard the sound of Fiona's shoes taking a tiny step backward. I hoped it was to run, and not just out of shock.

"Look, I don't care what you do with that asshole over there,"—he nodded his head my way—"and I don't even know who that other girl is, but you can't shoot Fiona. I won't let you do that."

"We could throw her off the side or something. You know, make it look like an accident, or suicide. Whatever," the guard I'd spared piped up. Both Nick and Jake turned to look, and he simply shrugged his shoulders. "Let me get my phone back first, though."

"Shut the fuck up, Tom," Nick shouted at him. He turned back to Jake, "let me handle her, okay?"

"Listen, Nick. I've spent far too long building this up just to let the whole thing collapse because you want to fuck that little redhead one more time," Jake said.

"You see?" I called out. "He's willing to do anything to keep this going. Makes me wonder what will happen to you, Nick, when you do something he doesn't like."

"Quiet! Do that again, and you'll wish we just shot you," Jake yelled over at me. It was too late, though; I could see it running through Nick's head. His mind might still be a little foggy from the alcohol, but I was getting through.

"Fiona, I..." he trailed off, and I could hear his heavy breathing from where I was standing. He mumbled a bit more, too low and slurred to make out. Whatever he said, it wasn't what they wanted to hear. Jake closed his eyes and grit his teeth, having finally reached a point where he could barely contain his frustration.

"Alright, Nick. You don't want me to kill her? Fine. Maybe she'll make a good first employee for our new brothel. The other one too, for that matter. Maybe I'll even let you have a go at her once for free before we open," Jake sneered, and his weaselly sidekick began to grin maniacally. I couldn't tell how serious his threat was, but it didn't matter; Nick punched him in the face, and chaos erupted on the other side of the landing as the guards struggled to pull him off.

"This is our chance. Go," I whispered, and the girls took off. I picked up the pistols and followed them down the tunnel. I glanced over my shoulder in time to see Tom the phone guard struggling in vain to get anyone's attention.

We kept running for who knows how long. I expected to hear them chasing behind us, bearing down, but the only sounds were the echoes of Melanie's bare feet striking the cold metal floors. We came up to one of the intersections that led back to the center and I signaled to the girls to stop.

"Which way do we go?" Melanie asked in a hushed tone. I glanced from one tunnel to the other. Going back through the central point seemed dangerous; if Jake and company managed to regroup, they might try to head us off through there. On the other hand, if they were chasing us down this much longer outer tunnel, it would give them more of an opportunity to catch up. No matter which way we headed, they'd be after us as long as we were in the tunnels. After realizing that, the solution was obvious.

I pulled up the blueprints and found another maintenance hatch like the one we'd entered through nearby. I waved to Fiona and Melanie. "This way."

We walked for a few minutes until I found the keycard door. It slid open on the first attempt, returning to the original frequency. Ascended wasn't operating out this far.

"Wait, what are we doing?" Fiona asked.

"The tunnels are too risky. If we head up to the surface, we might be able to lose them," I answered, ushering them through the hatch.

"Don't you think we might look a little too conspicuous walking around in the open?"

"We'll have to chance it." It slid shut behind us, and I fished the flashlight out of my pocket and turned it on. There were no glass shards around this one. As I stepped up to the exit, my fears were confirmed: the locks were still working over on this end. "Fiona, can you tell me anything about the locks on these?"

"Oh, uh… not really. Sorry, but the one we used has always just had a few loose bolts. They seem to break pretty quickly for whatever reason."

I scanned the perimeter with the flashlight until I found one of them. The bolts were stripped out, and the nuts just loose enough that I could twist them by hand. With the locking mechanism on this side of the door, it looked like it just might be doable. I emptied my pockets, stashed the confiscated guns in the corner, and handed my coat off to Melanie.

"This might take a little while, so go ahead and put that on."

"Are you sure?" she asked, and I nodded. Melanie sat down, knees up and huddled beneath it. As I worked on the lock, Fiona walked over.

"Lance… what do you think happened to Nick?" she whispered. I could sense how close she was standing, but I kept working.

"I honestly don't know."

"I didn't think—I mean, I was so sure that his feelings were just born out of possessiveness, you know? Wanting what he couldn't have. To think that all this time, maybe there was something more to it…"

"For the moment, let's just be glad he did what he did, and not worry about why."

Fiona returned to Melanie's side after that. I worked quietly for a while longer, keeping an ear out and running it over and over in my mind. I was certain now that I'd never be able to use a gun again; if a situation like that wasn't enough, nothing would be. And Jake didn't seem the type you could talk down. Nick had saved us, whether he knew it or not. I liked to think he did, that he'd managed a selfless act at last, even if it made me feel all the worse about it.

Jake's people never passed by, or if they did, I didn't hear them. When the lock finally came apart, I pushed it open, the chains on the outside just barely loose enough to let us slip through.

The cool evening air rushed over me as I climbed out of the tunnels. I pushed the hatch shut behind us as Melanie looked around in wonder.

"This is Magmell?" she asked. "Wow. The buildings up here are so beautiful. They're all fancy and stylish."

Fiona and I watched her wander, taking in this world that was all but alien. As she made her way out from the support, she caught sight of the park and ran off toward it. We followed slowly.

"It's grass. I've never walked on grass before. It's wet." Melanie pranced about like a fawn in the woods, enjoying her first encounter with nature, even if it was the carefully manicured kind. I glanced over at Fiona, who was almost as amazed by her reactions as Melanie was by the park.

I wanted to give her a chance, but It was already past three in the morning, and I was uneasy being out and about in Magmell so late at night. I turned to Fiona and quietly asked, "shouldn't we get moving?"

She sighed and brushed the hair out of her eyes, trying to compose herself.

"I, um… I'm not sure where to go. After what happened, I don't think Nick would tell them my address, but they could find it easily enough," she whispered back. "For all we know, they could be waiting there already."

It was hard to argue with that. My gaze shifted back to Melanie, who was on her knees examining the lilies bunched up near a tree trunk.

"Let's just let her savor this moment for now," Fiona said. "Who knows when she'll have this opportunity again?"

We watched her for a little longer, until a booming voice rang out of nowhere.

"Loitering in this area is strictly forbidden between the hours of eleven P.M. and seven A.M. Magmell Security has been notified and will arrive shortly."

"You've got to be kidding me," I muttered to myself. I spotted the domed cover of the security camera nestled high upon the streetlight. Fiona rubbed her temples for a moment.

"Of course." She sighed. "I'm sorry, I forgot all about these cameras. They're far more common on this end of Magmell than the eastern side."

"Is there any way we could sneak back into the maintenance tunnel until the coast is clear?"

"No chance. The cameras will be watching our every move until a guard arrives." As if on cue, the uniformed security agent rounded the corner of the path. He called out and Melanie froze, cowering under the tree. Fiona quickly tried to spruce herself up. "Let's hope I can talk our way out of this."

"Good evening, sir," she said, rushing over to intercept him.

"How are you doing?"

"It's a little late for a walk in the park, isn't it?" he asked, ignoring her greeting. "Can I see your resident I.D.?"

"Sure, one moment." He watched as Fiona retrieved her phone, and I took the chance to stash my gun in a bush. She opened the digital identification, then handed it over. He examined the screen for a moment, then tapped it against his own and looked over her file.

"Says here you've got one registered guest. I'm assuming that's you?" he asked as I approached.

"That's correct," I replied. Security agents, cops, guards— they're all the same. If you want to stay safe, you answer their questions and speak only when spoken to.

"So, who is this girl, then? A friend of yours?"

"She's my cousin," Fiona replied. "She just arrived in Kindred a few hours ago, so I haven't been able to register her yet. She just wanted to stretch her legs a little after a long flight."

"Right…" The agent looked at Melanie skeptically, struggling to her feet in the shabby coat and tattered nightgown. "Says here that you live over in the eastern quarter. Quite a walk, especially for someone without any shoes."

"Oh, that's because—well, you see…" Fiona trailed off.

"Yeah, that's about what I thought. I'm going to need all three of you to come with me."

"But there's no need for that," she said. Melanie's eyes darted back and forth, and she started wringing her hands, the anxiety of a life spent fearing authority clawing its way to the surface.

I leaned in and whispered in her ear, "that's enough. Let's just go with him."

Fiona glanced at me incredulously. "Alright. We'll come with you until we can straighten out this misunderstanding."

The security agent marched us to the nearest guardhouse. There was no actual jail inside—what use would Magmell have for one?—so they confiscated our things and locked us in a small conference room. I could only imagine how it would have gone if I still had those guns on me; something told me they wouldn't take it lightly. Fiona sat in the leather office chair, leaning onto the table and staring at a knot in its wooden surface.

"Well, now what?" she asked.

"It could be worse; at least here we're just bored. Getting captured might've been a blessing in disguise," I said. She sat up and looked at me.

"How so?"

"You said it yourself: they could have been waiting for us. Now we've got somewhere safe to hide out for the night." I leaned back against the wall across from her. "Maybe we can get in to talk to someone that can put a stop to Ascended's operations in the morning."

"You're right. I think I know just who to present our evidence to," she said. Fiona stood up and knocked on the door. The agent answered, and Fiona stepped into the hall to talk to him. Melanie sat in the floor nodding off. I knelt down and placed a hand on her shoulder.

"Hey, Melanie. You can go ahead and sleep in the chair if you want," I told her. She looked up, bleary eyed. "We'll handle things from here."

"Are you sure?" she asked, slowly getting up.

"Yeah. It's not the most comfortable, but you've slept on the floor enough already."

"Okay." It was that type of automatic response that can only come from someone slipping past the borders of consciousness. She laid back in the chair and pulled my coat over her. "Thank you. Good night."

She was out within seconds. I placed a finger to my lips as Fiona returned, then pointed over at Melanie. She closed the door quietly and sat down next to me on the floor.

"I think he'll see us, but he won't be in until nine at the

earliest," she whispered.

"Guess we have some time to kill, then," I whispered back. "I hope you don't mind that I gave her the chair."

"It's fine. I would have done the same anyway." Fiona slid forward and we sat in silence for a moment. If I was going to be held like this, at least it wasn't alone in the city jail.

"So what do they do when—" I started to ask, but grew quiet as Fiona's head came to rest on my shoulder.

# **Friday**

I awoke when the door opened, the security agent filling the opening as he passed through. Feeling surprisingly rested, I stood up and stretched, but my back made a persuasive argument against sleeping like that again.

"Mister Walsh is in, and he's willing to see you, Miss MacLeod," he said. Fiona blinked herself awake and I helped her to her feet. She ran her fingers through her hair, trying to make herself presentable. I woke Melanie, and she sat up with her eyes closed, moaning incoherently.

"Sorry to wake you up like this, but we've got to get going," I said to her. She let out a mighty yawn, looking as if she'd just been roused from a slumber that would give Rip Van Winkle a run for his money.

"It's okay." She rocked forward and stood, blinking her eyes a few times. Fiona walked out the door, but the agent stopped me.

"I tried to look up your file. There's no record of a Raymond Navarro in the database," he said.

"Isn't that odd?" I replied, and tried to pass through the door again. He placed a hand on my chest.

"What's your real name?"

"If you'll give me my phone, it will all make sense in a moment."

"Please, I need it if I'm going to convince Walsh about what's going on," Fiona said. The agent grunted and walked back to his desk. He retrieved both phones and handed them to Fiona.

"Here. The Steward is in the briefing room, through that door." The agent pointed two rooms down, toward the opposite side of the hall. "If you're wasting his time, he will be quite unhappy."

Inside sat a distinguished old man, his wrinkled face set against the flawlessly smooth fabric of his clothes. Gray hair wrapped around the sides of his otherwise bald head like a monochrome halo. His expression was a calm and patient one, but he looked like the sort of man that would give only as much time as he felt you needed and not a second more.

"Mister Walsh, there's something going on up here that you need to know about," Fiona said, sitting down at the conference table across from him.

"I knew your grandfather well, Miss MacLeod. He taught me quite a bit," Walsh said. "Regardless, that does not give you free reign to bring unregistered visitors into Magmell, and falsifying registration is not much better. Who are these two individuals? We'll start with the truth this time."

I stepped forward.

"My name is Lance Canela, and I'm a private investigator from the surface. I initially came here, with Fiona's assistance, to look for a missing girl. What we found in the process, however, must be addressed." I went on to elaborate about Ascended Employment and the smuggling of workers into Magmell. I showed him the recording of my talk with Jerrod, and the video Fiona had taken last night. Walsh listened intently, but he had a stone face that would have fit right in on Mount Rushmore. His reaction was impossible to gauge, even as Melanie related the tale of her journey from the lower floors to here. When at last we finished, Walsh remained silent for a brief eternity, contemplating the information we had presented.

"This is a very serious problem indeed," he stated at last. I was surprised to hear such a reasonable response. "But it must be handled with the proper care. I thank you for bringing it to my attention, and I shall handle it from here. A task force will be formed to locate and extradite all of the illegal workers at once."

"And what will you do about those who organized all this in the first place?" I asked.

"They will be placed on probationary status indefinitely. Should there be any further"—he placed finger and thumb to his chin, carefully considering his phrasing—"...indiscretions, they will be expelled from Magmell."

"You're kidding. That's it?" Melanie pushed forward, almost shouting. "They should be thrown in prison for the rest of their spoiled little lives!"

"We can't allow Magmell to suffer the kind of negative publicity a case against these young men would bring. The residents of Magmell value their peace and privacy above all else. I cannot jeopardize that." Walsh folded his hands and placed them gently on the desk.

"What if they try this again?" Fiona asked, placing a hand on Melanie's shoulder. She resisted at first, then relaxed.

"Now, now. Don't be ridiculous. After seeing how this turned out, why would they waste their time? And why would the people below fall for it again? They can't possibly be so thick," he said. Then, looking at Melanie, "no offense, my dear."

Her jaw dropped, while mine was so tightly clenched that I wasn't even sure I could pry it open to speak. Walsh paid us no heed. He stood up, and I knew that if he walked out the door, that would be it.

"But wait, what about the money the workers are owed for their time? The funds they were told they received, but never did?" Fiona asked, rising to her feet. Her words were pleading, desperate to find some some ray of hope in all of this.

"The contract they entered into is illegal and therefore unenforceable. It is unfortunate, but the workers are legally entitled to nothing." The security officer stepped into the room, and Walsh turned to shake Fiona's hand. "Thank you once again for informing me about this. We should be able to round up the remaining violators by the end of the week."

I couldn't say I was surprised. From the moment I'd set foot in Magmell, it was obvious that the people here cared only for their little world. If even Walsh couldn't be convinced to care about the exploitation of the workers, no one here would.

There was one last hope, a crime that he wouldn't be able to ignore. I'd only hoped to spare Fiona from hearing it.

"Mister Walsh, please. There's something else," I said. He glanced over, patience wearing thin. "These same men assaulted a Magmell resident last night. A young man by the name of Nick Irwin. Do you have his number on record?"

Walsh's expression soured, although I wasn't sure if it was towards me or Nick. "We have all residents on record."

"Contact him." A few seconds of silence passed. "Please."

His gaze shifted back to Fiona. Her composure cracked, eyes wide with the reminder of fear, but only for a moment. Walsh sighed and removed a phone from his pocket.

"If it will put an end to this, I'll call him myself." He held it to his face, volume loud enough that each ring pierced the silence of the room like a thunderclap. No one answered.

"It's hardly out of character for Mr. Irwin not to pick up," Walsh said, but his confidence had been shaken. He turned to the guard. "Keep them here for a little longer. Dispatch a security unit to the Irwin residence immediately."

Walsh and the guard headed back outside, leaving the three of us alone in a briefing room once more.

It was quiet in the room for a while, and boredom soon dragged Melanie back to sleep. Fiona was far too preoccupied for that, reliving the confrontation in the landing bay over and over.

"Be honest with me, Lance. Do you think they killed him?" she said at last. I'd known that question was coming since the moment Walsh left the room, and yet I still didn't have a good answer for it.

"Fiona… I can't say for sure. I don't have much experience with the kind of vile men we saw last night, outside of books. But based on what they said and how they behaved, and the kind of rage they'd managed to whip him into… well, I have a hard time seeing it go any other way. I'm sorry it had to be like this. I know—"

"That's all. Thank you for being honest with me," she replied flatly. I took the hint and shut up.

About an hour had passed from the time Walsh left to when the security guard returned. He announced that Nick Irwin was officially missing, and after paying a visit to the now-empty house that Ascended was operating from, that Jake Freely was the prime suspect. They recorded statements from each of us, one at a time. Walsh was nowhere to be seen.

"You're free to go," the guard said at last, as he brought Melanie back into the room. "You'll be escorted back to Miss MacLeod's apartment, and a pass for the young lady to return to the bottom will arrive shortly."

The guard handed over the rest of our possessions, and we left the building as soon as possible. The morning sun shone through the supports, almost disturbingly calm and pleasant. Conversation's absence made way for the unfamiliar songs of birds and the windswept rustling of the trees, as if the events of last night hadn't even happened. It wouldn't be long until they could no longer be kept a secret, and I could only hope more of Magmell's residents would be horrified than not. Some spark of humanity had to remain hidden here, or else what was the point of such carefully curated nature?

It was a long walk back, but the moment the guard dropped us off, I backtracked to pick up my gun. I wasn't planning on using it ever again, but it had still belonged to Grandpa, after all.

I returned to the apartment to find Melanie examining the

wallpaper, yet another of the many tiny luxuries which she'd never before seen. She looked back over her shoulder at me for a moment, standing there in her ripped and dirty nightgown, before resuming the path her fingers had traced over the patterns on the wall. Fiona emerged from the bathroom and handed her a set of soft, fresh towels. Melanie took them and shuffled past, as Fiona headed into her bedroom. I took a seat at the kitchen table and stared out at the midday clouds, rolling past the vibrant blues to which I'd never become accustomed.

I'd originally set out to help Mrs. Warner, and while I had accomplished that much, it hardly felt like a success. Was this just how it worked in real life? The bad guys kill people and then just skip town, never to be seen again? And I could only imagine what kind of repayment Wyatt might ask for. That was something I would just have to deal with that when the time came.

Fiona returned, carrying something that I couldn't see. She laid it out on the sofa before sitting down at the table next to me.

"Well, we did it. Didn't we?" she said. There was something odd about her tone that I couldn't quite place.

"Does it still count if they get away? If they always get away?" I asked. I took off my hat and set it on the table. There were a few new damaged spots I'd have to patch up when I got back home.

"I've been thinking about this a lot this morning. Nick's father was a powerful man. They didn't see eye to eye on most things, but I know he'll do anything to make the people that hurt Nick pay. I'm sure that's why Jake ran, and he won't be able to run forever." The thought wasn't as reassuring as it was meant to be.

"Guess all those people at the bottom of the Arcology owe him one. If it hadn't been for Nick, Ascended would've suffered little more than a slap on the wrist."

"I'm not sure how he'd feel about that. Probably just see it as an excuse to celebrate," she said, staring out the window.

"Look, Fiona…" I began, but she raised a hand.

"You don't have to say anything."

"I know that," I replied. "But I want to. You see, for me, dealing with some of the cases that I get... even the smaller ones, it's nothing but bad. I started this because I wanted to follow in my grandfather's footsteps, to help people like he did, but so often it just seemed like every person I met was awful. People as rotten as the world we're all stuck living in. And Nick, he seemed like just another of those awful people. But when it came down to it, he was willing to make a big sacrifice. I might not have liked him from what little I saw, but that's something I can respect. If even someone like Nick has redeemable qualities, then maybe the world's not too far gone just yet."

"Nick Irwin inspiring someone to believe in the good of the world," Fiona said, shaking her head with a smile. "I never thought I'd see the day."

The door to the bathroom clicked open, and Melanie emerged in her nightgown, hair still wet and flattened down around her head. Fiona stood up and walked over to the sofa to retrieve what she'd left earlier.

"Melanie, I thought you might like something else to wear. You shouldn't have to go home in that," she said, holding out a pair of black pumps and a silky blue dress, with the kind of flowing form and expert tailoring rarely seen on the cheap clothes available at the bottom of the Arcology. Melanie's jaw dropped instantly.

"No... I can't. I couldn't take that from you. It's too nice," she stammered. She looked so overwhelmed that I thought she might cry.

"Nonsense. I haven't worn this in quite some time." Fiona handed it off to her. "But it looks like it might fit you well. Don't you think it would be better for someone to get some use out of it?"

Melanie examined it with an awed reverence, stroking the lacy collar so lightly it seemed she wasn't quite sure it was real. Her concerned expression gradually melted into an adorable smile.

"Well, when you put it like that... okay. Can I try it on now?"

"Please, go ahead," Fiona replied. Melanie skipped back to the bathroom to change. I straightened my coat and played with my hat a bit, looking in every direction but hers. After everything we'd been through this week, I still wasn't sure what to say to her.

"Thank you, Fiona. For all your help, and for being so kind to a total stranger. I don't know what I would have done without your assistance," I managed at last. "It was never my intention to get you so involved, but... I'm glad you came along."

"I involved myself. You were a gentleman the entire time," she replied. I glanced over and our eyes met. "I was happy to help."

"Yeah." No, come on. She deserved a more meaningful response than that. "I think... Logan would be proud. A strong sense of justice runs in the MacLeod family blood, it seems."

"I don't know if I would go that far," Fiona scoffed. "But I appreciate the sentiment." The room fell silent again. "So... what are you going to do now?"

"Start looking for the next case, I suppose. You?"

"I'm not sure yet. There is one thing I am sure of, though: I can't continue living here. Not after everything I've seen."

"Yeah, I can understand that..." I said, a tinge of disappointment creeping through. No doubt she'd end up moving out to the country, or what little was left of it. It's the only place to get away from these kinds of problems nowadays.

"I'll see if I can find a place on the surface. I'm not quite ready to leave Kindred entirely."

"Oh." I kept my reaction subdued. "Perhaps we'll run into each other again, then."

"I'd like that." Fiona's cherry red lips shifted into a smile. "Although, I hope it's under better circumstances next time. I don't think I could handle this sort of thing every time we meet."

"Well—" I started, but I was interrupted by Melanie's entrance.

She stepped through the door, smooth legs first, followed by a wave of flowing navy fabric that accentuated the hips that I wasn't even sure she had a few minutes ago. The pure, clean white of the lace seemed all the brighter in contrast with her dark hair.

"What do you think?" she asked, grinning wide. She performed a dramatic twirl to show off all sides.

"It looks wonderful on you. I'm impressed with how well it fits." Her figure wasn't quite as full as Fiona's, but it was close enough to wear the dress.

"Yeah, it's quite lovely. I think your mother will like it, too," I agreed. Melanie pranced around a bit, making her way to the door.

"I'll never be able to thank you guys enough. No one… I mean, the bottom isn't a place where a stranger is gonna help you out very often."

"Part of the job, that's all," I replied. It's what Grandpa would say.

"It really is nothing." Fiona glanced at a clock on the wall. "The aerocar should be here any minute now. I'd hate to make him wait, especially after last night."

"Yeah. Shall we get going, Melanie?"

"Okay."

We stepped out into the hall and my phone chirped, announcing the arrival of Melanie's pass back into the Arcology. Outside, the aerocar was just settling in. Melanie gave Fiona a big hug, then climbed into the car. And then it was my turn. I looked back at Fiona, gazing into those discs of etched jade one last time.

"I'm… well…" I began. No, that's not how it's supposed to go. I steeled my resolve, then put an arm around Fiona's waist and pulled her into the deepest, most passionate kiss I could muster. It felt as though time stood still. It felt like an explosion of joy, like some kind of blissful bomb inside my head had gone off. Most of all, it felt like this was how we should part.

"Someday."

"Hopefully soon." Fiona was blushing. I turned around and walked to the car, the tails of my coat trailing off behind me in the breeze of the open pad. I closed the door, nodded to the driver and the aerocar took off.

"Thanks for your help last night, by the way," I said to him.

"Miss Fiona's nice. I don't mind helping her," he answered. "Besides, she certainly did make it worth my while."

I soon found myself back at the base of the Arcology, and with a few hours to spare. The guards at the checkpoint gave a few strange looks at Melanie's clothes, but eventually let us through. I left my belongings at the checkpoint and let Melanie lead the way.

The corner of M-22 was as dull and featureless as it had been the last time, but Melanie recognized it instantly. As we climbed the stairs outside of the flat gray building, I noticed she was growing anxious.

"What's wrong?"

"Nothing, just... how am I going to explain myself? She'll probably be so mad at me after all this," Melanie said, stopping at the top of the steps.

"I think you'll be surprised. I can tell you for a fact that she just wants to see you again, more than anything else." I pulled the door out, holding it open. "Darren, too."

"Darren... I should have listened to him." She sighed, looking off in the direction of the food bank. "Okay, let's go."

We walked down the hall to Mrs. Warner's door. I knocked on it twice, and shuffling sounds could be heard on the other side. The peephole went dark.

"Oh, are you the detective from the other day? Do you have some news?" she asked, shouting through the door.

"Yes, ma'am," I answered. Locks clicked and the door swung open, weak light pouring out into the darkened hallway. I stepped aside, and Melanie gave a hesitant wave.

"Melanie! You're okay," Mrs. Warner cried. She threw her arms out wide, as quickly as her feeble frame would allow. Melanie eagerly embraced her mother, a look of mild shock on her face.

"Mom… you're not mad?"

"Of course not." Tears seeped out, racing down her wrinkled skin until they landed on Melanie's dress. "I was so worried. You scared me, disappearing like that. You're all I have left, and the thought of losing you, too…"

"I'm sorry, Mom. I just wanted to help, but I knew you'd never let me go if I told you about it."

"I know, I know. It's okay. Just don't scare me like that again." She held Melanie's head close to her chest, petting her hair slowly.

"Sure thing," Melanie said in a muffled voice. She was sniffling too, struggling to hold back her own tears. Mrs. Warner looked over at me.

"And you, Mister Canela. I don't think I'll ever be able to repay you for this."

"You aren't supposed to, ma'am." It was a little embarrassing, somehow. "I'm just glad I was able to help."

Mrs. Warner stepped back and looked Melanie over, taking in her new outfit.

"And you've come back looking so beautiful, too! Where did you even get that?"

"A lot of things happened. It'll take a while to explain," Melanie replied bashfully.

"I'll leave you two to catch up, then. Farewell, Mrs. Warner. Melanie." I gave a little nod of acknowledgment and turned away.

"Thank you again," Mrs. Warner called out. Melanie repeated the sentiment, and I could hear the door swing shut behind me. I headed out of the building, back into the thick, foul air of the Arcology. The sun's light filtered through for its one brief visit of the day. Walking back to the checkpoint, it fell across my back, warm and powerful. Fiona's words sounded out in my head, reminding me that while it may have been a small victory, an incomplete victory, it was a victory nonetheless. I found who I was looking for this time, alive, and brought her home safe. I didn't even have to shoot anyone to do it. And in this world at the bottom, where the light is so rare, maybe brightening the life of an old woman is enough.

Keep reading for a special preview
of Lance Canela's next case:

# *EIDOLON*

## About the Author

A lifelong science fiction fan, Carlyle Edmundson is an up-and-coming young author. His debut novel, *The Arcology*, is the first in the Lance Canela series. He currently lives in North Carolina.

# Keep up with Carlyle

Visit retrophaseshift.com and join the mailing list to stay informed on new releases, appearances, exclusive insights into Lance's world, and more!

The boarded up window caved in with a splintering crash, exposing the bar to the light of day for the first time in a month. Bar stools had been smashed everywhere and the pictures on the wall were broken or missing outright. I pulled the plywood back far enough to climb inside the building that Wyatt had called homebase for as long as I'd known him. Shards of mirrored glass crunched under the thin soles of my shoes as I turned on the flashlight in my phone.

The place was abandoned, but the empty beer cans and broken bottles gathered at the base of the far wall made it clear that some local hoodlums had taken it over already. Best not to spend any more time here than I had to, but I needed to know what had happened to Wyatt. I walked past the bar, near a giant hole in the wall which had left pieces of drywall scattered over the floor. For a moment, I couldn't help but wonder what had happened to the bartender who had run this place; Wyatt had never made it clear just what their relationship was.

The short staircase leading up to the hacker's den was ripped apart, with the skeleton of the steps exposed. The door at the top was barely open, leaking hot, stale air down below. The frame bore the marks of forced entry, with the multitude of locks that Wyatt had always kept to cut him off from the outside world either mangled or outright missing. Inside, the room was barren, with nothing left to prove that tens of thousands of dollars of computer equipment had once been contained within. I couldn't tell if it had been stolen and pawned off or if Wyatt had simply relocated without notice, but the way the place was so thoroughly destroyed had me fearing the worst. I checked along the walls, searching for some clue that had been left behind, when my phone began to chirp loudly. I glanced at the screen to see a message transmitting.

"Took you long enough to come check on me, Lance!" Wyatt's voice came across the phone, crystal clear. The Sigil icon he used as his calling card glowed prominently on the screen. I looked around the room in confusion.

"I don't understand... where are you?"

"This is a limited interactivity message I've recorded for you before leaving. While I'm sure you're worried sick over me, I'm fine. Or at least, I was at the time I made this—which was twenty-seven days ago."

"What happened? Where did you go?"

"This message can't answer 'what happened,'" it replied. "I'll explain that in person. What I need you to do right now is to leave this room. There's a breaker panel on the outside of the building with a lock on it. You can find the key to it taped to the top of the third cabinet on the right, under the bar. Inside the panel, you'll find the device transmitting this message. Once you've retrieved it, you'll be given the next set of instructions." I stared at the icon, which now had a replay button visible. At least it seemed like Wyatt was okay. I put the phone back in my pocket and made my way down the stairs.

The area behind the bar had been trashed, probably by looters searching for any alcohol left behind. All the cabinet doors were open, and the taps had been broken off. An empty keg was wedged up underneath with a massive dent in the side. I was able to climb through the debris to the cabinet Wyatt had specified, which looked completely empty. I searched around the inside, carefully avoiding the splintered shelf until I found the key, tucked away above the rails of a drawer. I climbed back over the bar, then headed past the staircase to the back door. I had to ram my shoulder into it a few times to open it wide enough to get outside. More junk from inside the bar was piled up in the alley, broken tables and booths that had been dragged out to clear the way for whatever the hoodlums had been up to inside. I grabbed one of the metal rods from a barstool and propped the door open. The breaker box was a few feet down, near the edge of the building. I unlocked the box, and found a smooth, coin-sized device sitting at the bottom of the breaker stack. As I picked it up, the phone started to play messages again.

"You managed to find it? Alright, next step: pocket the transmitter. When you get home, tap it against your phone, and I'll send you instructions to find my new hideout." I marveled at the device for a moment, trying to figure out how it could possibly have been so reactive to my actions. I dropped it in the same pocket as my phone, to which the message cried out in response, "Hey! I said wait until you're home! I don't want anyone overhearing, you impatient dork."

I smirked and shook my head, then set off for home.

I returned to my apartment, phone already in hand as I walked through the door. Now that I knew he was still alive, my interest shifted from concern to a sort of bemused curiosity as to what he'd gotten himself into now. I sat down on the sofa, knees pressed up against the coffee table, which knocked against the shelf across from me. I tapped the device against the phone, and the message started to play once more.

"Alright, Lance, here's the last step: tomorrow, head to your office like usual. At 11:35 A.M., a taxi will pull up outside. Leave your phone upstairs and get in. I know it's locked down, but I can't risk anyone tracking your location and finding me that way. Once you're in the taxi, it'll take you to my new hideout. Don't miss it! I'm serious. Remember, you owe me. This transmitter will let me know when you arrive. See you then."

The message cut off. The last time I'd seen him, he'd tried to make a big deal about how busy he was, but it seemed like little more than his usual variety of posturing. Had there actually been something major going on? No wonder he was so keen on cashing in that favor.

I wouldn't find out until tomorrow morning regardless of how much time I spent thinking about it, so I decided to distract myself with one of my grandfather's old novels. I grabbed Raymond Chandler's *The Little Sister* off the shelf and settled in. Of course, it didn't matter how good the book was at this stage; as the hours passed, it grew harder and harder to focus, and Wyatt's absurd level of secrecy weighed all the heavier on my mind. I begrudgingly set it aside and tried to get some rest instead.

I got up in the morning and went through the same old ritual as any other day. Coat, hat, keys, book—the phone wouldn't be going far today, but one more item was on the list to replace it. I walked out the door without eating, setting off down the familiar path to my office. It was an old building, a far sight older than most in the neighborhood at this stage, but that was part of what had drawn me to it. I often wondered if, a hundred years ago, there had been some other private detective working out of it, with his name scrawled across the frosted glass in bold, black lettering instead of inscribed on a cheap plastic sign straight out of a 3D printer. Did he have all kinds of adventures? Or did he spend each week watching ambivalently as a different set of unfaithful spouses cheated themselves out of a divorce settlement? I certainly wouldn't be caught up doing that, but the rumbling of my stomach reminded me why he might.

The skies had turned a lifeless ash gray, the kind that served only to warn of the torrential rains that would follow shortly after. There were no shadows on a day like this; only the dull, uniform tint of scattered sunlight. My footsteps echoed throughout the empty stairwell as I climbed my way up. The office was peaceful this morning: no techno music from across the street, no cars passing by outside. That damned clock was still ticking away, each tick of the second hand dragged out for ten times that long. I sat down at my desk without bothering to remove my coat or hat, and pulled out the novel once more. It was back to waiting.

I must have checked out the window every five minutes for those next three hours, hoping to see a taxi pull up outside. When it finally did, I dropped the book and bolted down the stairs, jumping in before it even had a chance to stop. As I got myself settled in the backseat, I noticed the screens on the headrests of the front seats were displaying Wyatt's symbol instead of the usual map and payment information. I was quite impressed that he had actually taken over a cab just to meet with me.

The cab made its way to its destination slowly, and it soon

became clear why as I passed by the statue of Mayor Reinhold for the third time. The convoluted trail finally came to a halt in front of the Saint Arthur's Catholic Church in the eastern borough of Marsden, clear across town. While it had the look of a cathedral, it was actually one of the many smaller churches that had shuttered its doors in the last decade as they hemorrhaged believers to profit-oriented megachurches. Of course, that wasn't the only reason; a lot of people these days just didn't have much to thank their maker for. I walked up to the building and peered in through the stained glass windows, which had somehow managed to survive despite the building's abandoned state. I suppose the fear of God wasn't completely gone yet.

The inside still looked like a church, with row after row of pews that had a thick layer of dust resting undisturbed on them. As I stared, I heard a set of footsteps coming up behind. I spun around, ready to strike, until I recognized him as a familiar face. It was the bartender from Wyatt's old hideout, dressed in a loose windbreaker and sweatpants.

"Over here," he said, then walked off. I followed him around the corner to the building next door, which had a set of stairs leading down to a basement. He unlocked the door and waved me down, then led the way inside.

"So you had to move shop, too?"

"Yeah." He latched the door behind us and started walking down a narrow hallway to the left.

"And you're still with Wyatt, even after that?"

"Yeah."

"Mind if I ask why?"

"Yeah." We came up to another door, the bright mortar between the cement blocks giving away the fact that it was a recent addition. He shouted through the door, "He's finally here."

Bolts shifted and locks turned, and the door swung inward to reveal Wyatt's plump face.

"About time, Lance!" He snorted. For once, he wasn't wearing his Augmented Reality goggles, and I could see his eyes clearly for the first time since we'd met two years ago. His left eye had a patch of green in the lower right, quite distinct from the brown color that otherwise dominated it.

"Hey, the last thing you said to me was not to pay you a visit."

"And since when do you actually do what I tell you?" Wyatt backed up from the door, letting me inside. It was a much larger room than his previous hacker den had been; it had to be the basement of the church next door. He closed and locked it before taking a seat in front of the mindbogglingly expensive computer in the corner.

"Since you started sending cryptic texts like 'instructions to follow.'"

"Well shit, if I'd known that was all it took, I'd have done that from day one," he said. He rifled through a box nearby until he found the AR goggles and put them on. "Sorry, I still haven't had a chance to set up my rig properly yet. We packed it up so fast that I'm not sure where all the parts ended up."

"Yeah, I got that impression when I stopped by the bar yesterday. Are you planning on explaining just what the hell is going on, or am I just here on a social call?"

"Hey, you think you've been waiting around anxiously? Just imagine what the last three weeks have been like for me." He spun the office chair around toward me, staring up with a look far more serious than I'd ever seen him. "Alright, you might want to grab a seat for this. It's a long story."

I looked around and found a stool up against the wall. I carried it over and sat down in front of him.

"Well, let's get started."

***

When Wyatt is driven underground by the followers of a crusading hacker known only as Eidolon, Lance is saddled with the unenviable task of digging up dirt on them—which becomes even more off-putting when he has to partner up with a clickbait blogger whose only concern is the next big controversy. But as Lance gets to know Eidolon and what he stands for, he becomes less and less sure that he's on the right side. Is Wyatt merely taking advantage of him, or could there really be a dark secret at the heart of Eidolon's attempts to right the world?

Find out in *Eidolon*, now available from RetroPhaseShift!

www.ingramcontent.com/pod-product-compliance
Lightning Source LLC
Chambersburg PA
CBHW021105130626
46554CB00002B/547